"Don't say going to regret, Callie."

Ian placed his hand over her mouth. When she scowled at him, he removed his hand and said, "As I was saying before I was so rudely interrupted, I have never wanted a woman the way I want you. As furious as I am with you, I still want to haul you over to bed and make love to you. And you know it wouldn't be just a tumble. You also know what's happening between us is something special."

"Don't talk like that," Callie said roughly. "What is going on between us is not something special. It's happening because we're on the run. When this is all over and our lives are back to normal, we'll wonder what we ever saw in each other."

Ian gave a bitter laugh. "Lady, if you believe that, I have some swampland you might be interested in."

One night, suffering from insomnia,
Carin Rafferty turned on the television.
She got so excited watching professional
female pool players that she rushed to her
desk and by dawn, she had a rough
outline for *Sherlock and Watson*. For
several weeks, she haunted pool parlors,
grilled pool players of all ages and read
every book she could find on the subject.
By the time she sat down at the
typewriter, she felt as if Callie and Ian, her
heroine and hero, had taken her cue and
written their own story.

Watch for Carin's next Temptation novel,
Christmas Knight, in December.

Books by Carin Rafferty

HARLEQUIN TEMPTATION
281—I DO, AGAIN
319—MY FAIR BABY

HARLEQUIN AMERICAN ROMANCE
320—FULL CIRCLE
359—A CHANGE OF SEASON

Sherlock
and Watson
CARIN RAFFERTY

Harlequin Books

TORONTO • NEW YORK • LONDON
AMSTERDAM • PARIS • SYDNEY • HAMBURG
STOCKHOLM • ATHENS • TOKYO • MILAN

With love to my aunt, Charlene Gilman,
my best friend and soul mate

Published September 1991

ISBN 0-373-25463-6

SHERLOCK AND WATSON

1

WHEN THE FRONT DOOR of Kelly's Pool Parlor opened, Ian Sherlock lifted his head and glanced up warily. He tightened his grip on his cue, but relaxed it after an attractive blonde sauntered into the dingy, smoke-filled room and headed for the bar. He was disappointed that she wasn't Doc Watson. But then again, she could have been a police officer!

Relieved, Ian returned his attention to the pool table, forcing himself to concentrate on the balls spread across the green felt. The police wouldn't look for him here, he assured himself. He wasn't known for hanging out in pool halls. But he wasn't normally known as a bail jumper, either. That nagging reminder made him miss the nine ball. *Damn!*

He concentrated on the ball again. But just as he was ready to make the shot, a sultry voice drawled, "You'll never sink it from that angle."

Ian raised his eyes and found himself staring at enough cleavage to give him pause. Only after the woman released a throaty laugh did he force his gaze upward. At close range, the blonde was more than attractive—she was downright gorgeous. Her honey-blond hair was feathered around her oval face and stopped just below her jawline, emphasizing the allure of her full lips. Her long, tousled bangs accented her blue eyes. Her nose was slightly turned up at the end, giving her a mischievous look. He then lowered his gaze. Her figure—encased in a clingy red silk blouse with a plunging neckline and a pair of skintight black denims—was most definitely wolf-whistle material.

Ian had never been averse to spending time in the company of a good-looking woman—even if she was dressed a little bawdily and looked too hard-edged for his taste. Also, she'd be the perfect distraction until the mysterious Doc Watson arrived, and the perfect cover if the police raided the place. They were searching for a single man, not a couple. If worse came to worst, he could always pull her into his arms for a kiss. There wasn't a man alive—even the most dedicated cop— who'd interrupt another man's clench on a body like that.

He gave her his best roguish smile and said, "Five bucks says I can make it."

She pursed her lips. "You're on."

"Show your money."

She reached into her bosom and pulled out a five-dollar bill. Then she ran it between her fingers to smooth it and tapped it against the edge of the table. She performed the act so swiftly that Ian arched a brow. He couldn't prevent himself from staring at her high, rounded breasts, wondering just how much money was stored in her décolletage and if she had a filing system for denominations.

"I'm showing mine. It's time to show yours," the woman told him.

Ian blinked at her overt sexual innuendo. Since her big blue eyes were wide with innocence, he left the line alone—though his tongue twitched with a dozen X-rated comebacks. He cleared his throat and reached for his wallet. "The smallest bill I have is a ten."

She leaned across the table and extended the five. "Your change."

Ian knew it was crazy, but just the thought of touching her money—which had been so intimately acquainted with her a moment before—sent a rush of hot-to-trot hormones through his bloodstream.

"We could sweeten the pot," he suggested, fearing that if he took the five he might be tempted to do something unorthodox with it, and he was already in enough trouble. He didn't need a charge of sexual perversion in a public place added to the police's growing list of complaints against him.

She straightened slowly, and Ian braced the cue between his feet as he avidly watched the five disappear back into her bosom and a ten replace it. She *definitely* had a filing system, and boy, would he love to do an audit of her funds.

"Let's see your stuff," she urged.

Ian nearly choked as he gallantly suppressed the witty retorts that sprang to his lips. He then bent over the table, trying his best to look in control of the game. The truth was he'd never been more than a fair pool player, and she was most likely right—he'd never sink the nine ball from this angle. Nor could he afford to lose the ten.

But even as his common sense advised him to call off the bet, his macho ego insisted that it was better to be reduced to lunch money than to renege on the bet—especially when the woman had provided him with such an enticing floor show.

He tented his fingers, squinted at the ball and held his breath as he made his shot. When it dropped into the pocket, he let out a low whoop of triumph.

"I'm impressed," the woman said. "You must be a pro."

Ian would have sworn there was a touch of irony in her voice. But he couldn't find anything in her expression to confirm it. "I'm strictly an amateur. Making that shot was pure luck."

"The oldest hustle line in the world," she stated dryly as she tossed her ten-dollar bill to the center of the table.

"Keep the money," Ian told her.

She looked ready to protest, then nodded in agreement. "How about if I buy you a beer instead?"

Ian started to refuse, knowing that he shouldn't imbibe. He needed to be clearheaded when he finally found Doc Watson. But one beer wouldn't incapacitate him, and maybe the woman could give him some information about Watson. After all, he was claiming he owed Doc money. He should at least be able to identify him.

"Only if you agree to join me," he answered.

"Sure." She turned toward the bar. "Hey, Mick. Two drafts, and put it on my tab."

"You must play a lot of pool if you run a tab," Ian remarked as he followed her to a rickety table at the back of the room, his eyes focused on the natural sway of her posterior. The rear view was as good as the front.

"I do," she replied as she sat down.

Ian sat across from her. "You know all the regulars?"

"Every one of them."

The bartender arrived with the beer and set the glasses on the table. He shot Ian a glowering look before saying to the woman, "Everything okay?"

"Everything's fine, Mick," she assured him.

"It looks as if you have a bodyguard," Ian commented when the bartender walked away.

She cast a fond glance toward the burly man's back. "Mick's an old friend. So tell me, Mr. —"

"Sherlock," Ian provided. "Ian Sherlock. You can call me Ian."

"Okay, Ian. What brings you into our little neighborhood pool parlor?"

Ian leaned back in his chair and took a sip of beer, hoping the nonchalant pose would disguise his baldfaced lie. "A debt. I played a few games with Doc Watson last week, and he beat the socks off me. Since I didn't have enough to cover our last wager, he told me to bring it here."

"You must know Doc pretty well if he let you carry an I.O.U."

There was that touch of irony in her voice again, but it still wasn't reflected in her face. She'd make a hell of a poker player. "Actually, Doc is a friend of a friend."

"Oh. Who's this mutual acquaintance?"

Ian hesitated, wondering if he dared mention Quincy McKiernan's name. The man was on the run, and Ian knew that Quincy and Doc were thick as thieves. He'd listened to Quincy rattle off a hundred tales of his and Doc's escapades as pool hustlers. He should have known then that he couldn't trust the man. He was convinced that if anyone knew where Quincy was hiding, it would be Doc. However, if Doc found out Ian was looking for Quincy, he'd most likely clam up or—worse—disappear.

"Quincy McKiernan," he replied, taking a chance. She might have seen Quincy recently, and maybe, just maybe, have information on where he could be found. "Do you know him?"

"Everyone knows Quincy. He's Doc's best friend."

"Yeah," Ian said. Trying to sound casual, he continued, "I'm surprised Quincy hasn't been in today. To listen to him talk, you'd think he lived here."

"Really?" She ran a finger around the rim of her glass before saying, "That's odd, because Quincy rarely visits Kelly's. Two pros in the same parlor isn't good for business."

Great! He'd just made his first major mistake! He'd better change the subject quick before he blew his cover. That kind of mistake could mean the difference between freedom and a few decades in prison.

"By the way, I didn't catch your name," he prompted as he raised his glass to his lips and took a healthy swig of beer.

She gave him an enigmatic smile and announced, "Watson, Dr. Calandra Watson. Considering that you owe me money, you can call me Doc."

CALLIE GREW CONCERNED when Ian began to choke on his beer and gasp for breath. She leaped up from her chair and began to pound on his back.

After his choking spasm subsided, Ian hoarsely exclaimed, "My word, woman! Stop beating on me before you break my back!"

"I was just trying to help," she said as she returned to her seat. "Are you okay?"

"Choking to death is one of my favorite pastimes," he grumbled. "Why didn't you tell me you were Doc instead of letting me make a fool of myself?"

"I hadn't had a good laugh today," she answered with a grin. "What's Uncle Quincy done this time?"

"*Uncle* Quincy?" Ian responded. "You're related to that thief?"

Callie stiffened. "He's my mother's brother, and he's *not* a thief."

"The hell he's not. Because of him, I'm about to land in jail!"

Callie shook her head. "Uncle Quincy sometimes walks a fine line when it comes to the law, but he never crosses over it. If you think he's done something wrong, I can assure you that you're mistaken."

"Yeah? Well, tell that to the district attorney who wants to throw the book at me, the bail bondsman who holds the title to my business and the hanging judge who's just itching to string me up. Your uncle framed me, lady. If I don't find him, I'm going to be mailing lifetime change-of-address cards," Ian explained in a furious whisper.

Callie rubbed her jaw in an effort to soothe the sudden throbbing in her bottom left wisdom tooth. As usual, her cavity-free teeth only ached when her uncle was in trouble. If the intensity of the pain she was now feeling was any indication, Quincy was in *big* trouble.

"I'm sure you're wrong, Mr. Sherlock. Even if Uncle Quincy did break the law, he wouldn't let someone else be punished for it. He's too honorable for that."

"Honorable?" Ian scoffed. "Six months ago your uncle showed up at my office begging for a job. His clothes were in rags. His shoes had holes in them. I didn't need any more help, but I felt sorry for him, so I hired him. Now my wardrobe is about to consist of prison blue. I'd hardly call that honor!"

"The hustle," Callie mumbled in resignation.

"What did you say?" Ian asked suspiciously.

Callie gave him a weak smile. "He hustled you. Every couple of years Uncle Quincy gets a burning desire to hold down a regular job. He puts on his 'penniless' suit and shoes and cons someone into hiring him."

"Why doesn't he fill out an application form like everyone else?" Ian asked sarcastically.

Callie's smile grew weaker. "He eventually gets tired of working and quits without notice. Employers tend to frown on that habit."

"In other words, he can't get a good recommendation from a previous employer."

"Yes. But it really isn't fair. While he's working, he does a good job."

"He just quits without notice."

Callie shrugged, then explained. "He's a pool hustler. Eventually the lure of the tables becomes too powerful to ignore."

"And he can't ignore it long enough to give a two-week notice?"

"It's hard to understand."

Ian muttered something that sounded suspiciously rude. "Where is he?"

"I don't know," Callie said. "I'm telling the truth," she added when he scowled at her.

"You haven't heard from him at all?"

Callie squirmed on her chair as she studied Ian Sherlock's angry face. He was a handsome man with the lean build of a swimmer. It looked as if he hadn't shaved in a couple of days. His clothes were visibly more rumpled than an average day's worth of wear would warrant. He wore his light brown hair short at the sides and brushed it back from his broad forehead. His eyes were almost as blue as her own. His jaw was square, his nose straight and narrow.

"There was a message from him on my answering machine," she finally confessed.

"What did it say?"

"Nothing that made any sense," she hedged.

"What did it say?" Ian repeated firmly.

"That he'd found the end of the rainbow, and when he wrested the pot of gold from the little people, he'll give me a call."

Ian gaped at her. "What in hell does that mean?"

"Probably that he'd been on a toot," Callie offered.

"He's a drunk as well as a thief?"

"He's not a drunk or a thief. He's . . . Well, he's just Uncle Quincy."

Ian ran his hand through his hair. "Look— Hell, I can't call you Doc. What's your name again?"

"Calandra. You can call me Callie."

"Yeah. What kind of doctor are you, anyway?"

"I have a Ph.D. in botany."

"You're a flower child?"

"I'm a woman, not a child, Mr. Sherlock," she corrected in her sternest professorial tone.

His blue eyes scrutinized her, and Callie shivered. It wasn't an unpleasant sensation—just disturbing.

"Sure. You're Mother Nature in all her glorious splendor. How do I find Quincy?"

"If he doesn't want to be found, you won't find him."

He regarded her thoughtfully. Callie stared back. Meeting those piercing blue eyes was becoming harder by the minute. She could almost hear the wheels turning inside his head and knew he would eventually come to the logical conclusion. It happened much sooner than she'd anticipated, indicating that the man was far more intelligent—and ultimately more dangerous—than his disheveled appearance indicated.

"If I can't find him, you can, can't you?"

"I'm not sure. I've never tried to find him."

"You probably could if you tried."

"I'm not sure," Callie insisted. "Even if I could, why should I look for him?"

"To save an innocent man—namely me—from going to prison," he retorted.

"And why should I believe that you're innocent and not merely attempting to frame my uncle?" she countered. "Forgive me, Mr. Sherlock, but I've known my uncle all of my life, and he's never given me cause to believe that he'd actually break the law. You, on the other hand, I've known for about twenty minutes, and our acquaintance began with a lie."

Ian felt his temper flaring, but he controlled it. Callie's loyalty to her uncle was admirable, if frustrating.

Intuition told him to opt for total honesty if he wanted her help.

"You're right, Callie. I did lie. But I'm a desperate man. My life is collapsing, and your uncle is the only person who can save me."

"What is it that you've supposedly done?" Callie asked.

Ian gave her a grim smile. "I own a chain of salvage yards that specialize in rare and antique auto parts. Last week, I was arrested for grand theft auto. I'm being accused of running a car-theft ring and a chop shop to supply my specialty parts."

Callie let out a low whistle. "That sounds serious."

Ian nodded. "I'm also charged with interstate trafficking of stolen cars, as well as shipping stolen merchandise through the mail."

Callie gulped. "Aren't those federal offenses?"

"Let's just say that I wouldn't be surprised to find myself on the FBI's Most Wanted list tomorrow."

"But that's only for dangerous felons on the loose, and you just said that you've been arrested."

"I've skipped bail."

"You're wanted by the police?" she gasped.

"Not so loud," Ian muttered irritably as he cast a glance around the room. The smoke was so heavy now that he could barely see the bar. The crowd had grown to the point where the din had risen to a low roar. If anyone had heard her, they had to have superhuman hearing. "Do you really hang out in this place?"

"Yes, I really *hang out* in this place," Callie answered. "You have to turn yourself in, Ian. Skipping bail is—"

"If I do that, I won't be able to prove I'm innocent," Ian interrupted with aggravation.

"So, hire a private investigator."

"Callie, if your life was on the line, would you trust it to someone you didn't even know?"

"We aren't talking about my life. We're talking about yours."

"Exactly."

Callie gave a frustrated shake of her head. "When the police catch up with you, they'll lock you up and throw away the key. If you turn yourself in, the judge will most likely be lenient and you'll have a chance to find out who framed you. Believe me, you won't be able to do that from a jail cell."

"You really believe I'm innocent!" he exclaimed in surprise.

"Well, of course I believe you're innocent," she muttered. "A guilty man wouldn't come charging in here, tell me a wild story like this, and then confess that he's skipped bail. Besides, Uncle Quincy would never work for a crook."

"When it comes to your uncle, you're blind, aren't you?"

"Not at all," Callie denied vehemently. "I'm very aware of all his foibles and faults. I also owe him my life."

Ian frowned. "I wish you hadn't said that."

"Why?"

"Because now I can't trust you. A woman who owes a man her life is not a woman who'll search for the truth."

Callie shot to her feet, braced her hands on the table and leaned forward until her nose was nearly brushing his.

"That, Mr. Sherlock, is the most asinine statement I've ever heard," she declared in a furious tone. "Caring about someone does not demand blind obedience.

"Yes, I owe Uncle Quincy my life," she continued. "He also taught me some very important lessons—the major one being that there is nothing more sacred than freedom. He wouldn't knowingly steal away your freedom, any more than he would steal away mine. If he's on the run, there's a reason. I'm going to find out what it is."

"*We* will," Ian corrected, feeling a sudden urge to close the short distance between them and kiss her. There was fire in her, and where there was fire, there was also passion. Still, his life and freedom was in her hands so he restrained his libido.

"What does 'we will' mean?" Callie demanded.

"That, Dr. Watson, means that from this moment on, you and I are going to be as close as Siamese twins. Where you go, I go—until we find good old Uncle Quincy."

Callie drew back in horror. "I'm not cavorting all over the countryside with a wanted man. I could end up being arrested for aiding and abetting!"

There was a wicked gleam in Ian's eyes as he drawled huskily, "Honey, the last I heard, there was no law against 'cavorting' in the state of Pennsylvania."

Callie couldn't believe it. Ian Sherlock had her flustered! Good heavens, she hadn't been flustered in so many years that she didn't even know how to handle it. Since the age of thirteen, she'd practically lived in the world of pool halls and had learned to give as good as she got.

"Mr. Sherlock, grow up," she snapped as she whirled away from the table and marched toward the door. Siamese twins! And as for cavorting with him? Well, she'd rather be staked out on an ant hill.

It wasn't that Callie actually had anything against men. She *liked* men. They were enjoyable to visit with, but she was always relieved when they went home.

"From now on, we're Siamese twins," Ian reminded as he caught up with Callie and linked his arm with hers. "Where you go, I go."

"Mick might take exception when you accompany me into the ladies' room," she remarked sweetly, veering in that direction. "You should have come in drag."

"I don't like shaving my legs," Ian explained with a teasing laugh. "All that hair just grows back."

"We women have to suffer such indignities, don't we?"

"Yes, we do," he taunted in a mock falsetto. Then his voice lowered. "Make sure you have to use the facilities, Callie, because I swear I'm going in with you. I don't want to fight with Mick over nothing."

"He's bigger than you are."

"The bigger they are, the harder they fall."

"You wouldn't lay a hand on Mick!"

"Are you willing to risk five smackers on that bet?"

She came to an abrupt halt and scowled at him. "I never bet on games of violence, only on games of skill."

"Normally, I share that sentiment," Ian announced. "However, Dr. Watson, I have been pushed into a new game with new rules. I'm innocent. I plan to stick to you like glue until you help me find Quincy so I can prove it. Even at the price of my own life."

Suddenly chilled, Callie backed away from him. "You don't mean that."

"Yes, Callie, I do," he said so quietly that his words rang true. "I'd rather die than do time for a crime I didn't commit."

"That's a foolish philosophy."

He shrugged nonchalantly. "Then I'm a fool."

"It just so happens that the cop on this beat is a good friend of Mick's, and he stops by every afternoon for a cup of coffee. If there's a warrant out for your arrest, you could be in serious trouble in just a few minutes."

"Then it's up to you to make sure that doesn't happen, isn't it? It only seems fair that you protect me. After all, your uncle got me into this mess in the first place."

"Uncle Quincy didn't frame you!" she exclaimed.

"Then help me find him so you can prove that."

"I've told you I don't know where he is."

"But you can find him, Callie."

"What am I going to do with you?" she demanded angrily.

"Take me home and feed me?" he offered hopefully. "I haven't had a decent meal in forty-eight hours. And as for showering..."

Callie wrinkled her nose. "Say no more. I get the picture." She surveyed his rumpled shirt and jeans with obvious distaste. "I don't suppose you have a change of clothes?"

He grinned, and Callie didn't like the lustful gleam in his eyes. "No, but I do have a knack with towels."

"A woman never really appreciates her nice, quiet life until she's faced with adversity," Callie muttered under her breath, annoyed by the provocative image of Ian Sherlock in a towel. She wasn't prone to fantasy—sexual or otherwise. Her uncle was going to pay dearly for this invasion. "Let's go home. I want you to know that I don't tolerate beard stubble in my sink. You shave, you clean. Even Uncle Quincy obeys that rule."

"I'll be the perfect guest," Ian promised, raising his hand in a boy-scout salute. Callie didn't believe one word of his vow.

But having him in sight was preferable to having him searching for Quincy on his own. He might find him before she did, and she couldn't let that happen. She knew her uncle was innocent. However, it was clear that he was on the run. That meant he probably knew who was responsible for Ian's troubles. Knowing her uncle as well as she did, she was certain he was working on some outrageous scheme to save the day. Unfortunately, his schemes had a tendency to blow up in his face.

They silently walked toward her car. As she drove to her apartment, she rubbed her jaw. This was undoubtedly the worst toothache she'd had in her entire life.

2

QUINCY had been expecting the call. That didn't stop him from jumping out of his skin, though, when the phone rang. He tensed as it rang the obligatory two times before going dead. If the caller was Devon Halloran, he would phone back and let it ring three times before hanging up. Then, there would be a third call right on the heels of the second one. Quincy was supposed to pick up on the fourth ring of the third call. He hated this cloak-and-dagger business.

He cursed as he paced the claustrophobic motel room where he was hiding out. Was this how Callie had felt when she'd spent that year as a guest of the state? The thought sent bile rushing to Quincy's throat, and he swallowed it down with effort.

Callie. Blessedly sweet, vulnerable Callie, who had a chip on her shoulder the size of Alaska. He continued pacing and scooped up the phone on the fourth ring of the third call.

"Halloran?"

"Quincy, you know we aren't supposed to use surnames," Devon Halloran hissed. "What if the telephone is tapped?"

"Devon, hang up your trench coat and put a hold on your Sam Spade imitation," Quincy barked. "You know this phone isn't tapped."

"It's only prudent that we take precautions."

"Been studying the dictionary again?" Quincy mocked. "I didn't know you'd made it as far as the *p*'s. *Prudent* and *precautions* in the same sentence? Webster would be proud."

"Stuff the sarcasm, McKiernan."

"I thought we weren't supposed to use surnames."

"We aren't, so stop rattling my railings."

"The saying is 'rattling my cage,'" Quincy corrected, shaking his head in exasperation. "What did you find out about Callie and Ian Sherlock?"

"The suspect connected with the subject this afternoon."

"Damn," Quincy muttered softly. "Me and my big mouth really did it this time. If I hadn't babbled on about my escapades with Doc, Ian Sherlock would have never hooked up with her. Why couldn't I have kept my trap shut for a change?"

"Because you're a braggart?" Devon suggested.

With anyone else, Quincy would have taken offense at such a statement, which smacked of censure. Devon didn't have enough brains to be censorious. Only a fool would entrust him with not only his life, but that of his beloved niece. Yeah, a fool like himself.

Still, whatever Devon lacked in brain power was more than made up for in devotion. A dog couldn't have been a better friend to Quincy, and Devon was besotted with Callie. Considering their twenty-five-year age difference, it was love from afar, as it should be. Quincy knew that Devon would lay down his life for Callie.

"What happened when they met?" he asked, hoping that his worst fears hadn't been realized—that Ian Sherlock hadn't blurted out his story, or if he had, Callie had told him to take a hike.

Devon blithely delivered the bad news. "They talked. Then the subject took the suspect home with her."

Quincy groaned. Alone, Ian Sherlock wasn't a threat. Teamed with Callie, who was the only person in the world who could track him down, the man became as dangerous as a stick of dynamite. Quincy had worked too hard setting up this hustle to prove Lincoln Galloway's innocence. If Ian found him, he'd screw it up and they'd all end up in jail for a very long time.

What to do next? If only the police hadn't stumbled across his operation, he would have had this entire mess resolved and the crooks would be in jail. He'd seen their guns and knew they didn't carry them for show.

Now Callie would be looking for him. Since the crooks were also looking for him, it was quite possible—no, make that probable—that their paths would cross. If they learned that Callie was his niece, they'd use her to get back the ledgers he'd stolen from them. Quincy wasn't foolish enough to believe that if he returned the ledgers, they'd just let him and Callie walk away.

Though he'd considered calling her and telling her what was going on, it was far too dangerous to risk her becoming involved. He had to make sure that Callie was safe, and there was only one way he could think of to guarantee her safety: he was going to have to turn her and Ian in to the police. In the company of Ian, Callie would be in violation of her parole and she'd be sent back to jail.

"So, should I set up a stakeout?" Devon asked.

"No," Quincy answered grimly. "Get over here. I need to deliver a message."

He knew that he was about to become one more traitor in his niece's life and she would end up hating him. But he had to put her back in jail or she might walk into a situation that could get her killed.

He scrawled a note and stuffed it into an envelope. Glancing around his ten-by-ten room, he began wondering if jail and death weren't one and the same.

"I'm sorry, Callie," he whispered miserably, "but I'm too far into the hustle to back out now."

IAN TOLD HIMSELF it was rude to snoop, but that didn't stop him from opening Callie's bedroom door a crack and peeping inside when he emerged from the bathroom.

Like the rest of her apartment, it wasn't what he'd expected. Considering the outlandish clothes she'd been wearing at the pool hall, he'd expected her home to be garish. Instead it was decorated in subdued earth tones and pastels. She also had enough plants to open a flower shop.

"If I'd known you had such a bad sense of direction, I would have drawn you a map to the guest room," Callie drawled behind him.

Ian spun around in surprise and cursed the guilty blush heating up his cheeks. "I'm sorry, Callie. I was being nosy. It won't happen again."

Callie couldn't decide which was more disconcerting—Ian's straightforward confession of snooping or his impressive hair-covered chest. Her eyes skimmed over him, taking in every detail from the top of his shampooed head to the tips of his scrubbed toes. He was right. He did have a knack with towels. She ignored the quivering sensation that skidded over her skin, and thrust a robe at him.

"My neighbor was kind enough to loan you his robe so I can wash your clothes. While you put it on, I'll fix you something to eat. After that, we'd better go buy you a few changes of clothing."

"I can't go shopping," Ian reminded her as he accepted the garment and tossed it over his shoulder.

"Oh, that's right," Callie mumbled, straining to look anywhere but at him. Why didn't he put the darn robe on instead of standing there imitating Tarzan in a loincloth? "You're a wanted man. You can give me your sizes, and I'll pick up the clothes."

"I can't do that, either."

Callie impatiently crossed her arms over her chest. "And, pray tell, why not?"

"I can't afford to buy any clothes. I only have twenty dollars on me. By now the police are probably waiting for me to use my checking account or credit cards so they can get a fix on my whereabouts."

"You went on the lam with only twenty dollars in your pocket?" Callie gasped.

"No. I had thirty dollars, but I had to give ten to the truck driver who drove me to King's Creek."

"If this is your example of planning, I'm surprised you stayed in business long enough to be accused of a crime," she said, amazed. "Good heavens, Ian, even a kid running away from home has enough sense to take his piggy bank with him."

He had the grace to look sheepish. "I didn't plan to skip bail, Callie. It just sort of happened."

"It just *sort of* happened?" she repeated incredulously. "How does skipping out on your bail just *sort of* happen?"

"Well, I knew the best way to find Quincy was to find Doc, so I started going to all the pool halls in Harrisburg looking for you," he explained. "Everyone had heard of Doc Watson, but no one seemed to know where Doc was hanging out these days. Finally, some man referred me to a pool hall in a neighboring town and told me to talk to Dynamite Dan."

"Well, I'll be darned!" Callie exclaimed. "I haven't seen Dynamite in ages. How is he?"

"He's great. He said to give you his best," Ian told her. He now understood Dynamite Dan's malicious smirk when he'd directed him to Kelly's. Ian had believed he was simply being sent on another wild-goose chase. In actuality, he was being set up. Come to think of it, everyone he'd talked to had to have known that Doc was a woman, but no one had had the courtesy to enlighten him. That "closed club" attitude had convinced him that without her help, he'd never find Quincy.

He continued. "Dynamite told me to check out Kelly's in King's Creek. I headed back to my car, but some old woman had backed into it and called the police. By the time I arrived they were calling in my license plate number, so I had to run."

"Ian, I think you left out some important detail in this story," Callie suggested. "Just exactly why did you have to run?"

"Because they were calling in my license plate number."

"What does that have to do with anything?"

"A condition of my bail was that I wouldn't leave the city limits of Harrisburg. As soon as they learned who owned the car, they were going to find out that I wasn't supposed to be there. That meant my bail would be revoked. As you so aptly stated earlier, I sure can't prove my innocence from a jail cell."

Callie shook her head. "That story is too absurd not to be true. Have you always had such bad luck?"

"No. My bad luck started the day I hired your thieving uncle."

Callie had a feeling his gibe was partially true. Quincy created mayhem wherever he went. The worst part was he never did it intentionally.

"Lucky for you, I'm flush right now. I can give you a loan."

"I'll pay you back, Callie."

His words made her insides feel like marshmallow. He'd spoken with such sincerity, and Callie's life revolved around the insincere. Her tooth began to throb again, and she rubbed her jaw.

"Callie, what's wrong?"

She looked up, startled to discover Ian standing inches away from her.

"Wrong?" she repeated inanely, unable to tear her eyes away from his bare chest. It was so broad, and the thicket of hair covering it so enticing. She had to curl her hands into fists to keep from touching him—especially after her nose received a dose of freshly shampooed-and-showered man.

"You keep rubbing at your jaw as if you were in pain."

Before she could respond, he reached out and lifted her hair away from her face. She didn't know if the tears in her eyes were caused by his tender touch as he gently examined her jaw or by the concern etched on his face. It had been so long since anyone had shown her such consideration.

"I just have a toothache," she mumbled.

His concerned look deepened. "Have you seen your dentist?"

Callie released a brittle laugh. "My dentist can't help me. This is an Uncle Quincy toothache."

Ian dubiously regarded her. "An Uncle Quincy toothache?"

"Whenever he's in trouble, I get a toothache."

"Then you must get a lot of toothaches."

"I do not!" she denied angrily, stung by his words. "You may not believe this—he really is a decent man."

Ian released his hold on her hair and ran his hand over it in a soothing gesture. "Calm down, Doc. For what it's worth, until I was arrested, I thought so, too."

"Why are you so convinced that it was Uncle Quincy who set you up? Why aren't you suspicious of any of your other employees?" she asked in agitation. "He wouldn't do this to you. I know he wouldn't."

She looked so upset that Ian wasn't sure he should answer her questions. It was clearly apparent that she adored her uncle, which meant she might take his information and run. When she found Quincy, they'd disappear and Ian would never find the man. He couldn't let that happen.

His resolve began to waver. He could have ignored the pleading expression on her face that was begging him to tell her it was all a mistake. He could even have ignored the pain and confusion reflected in her big blue eyes. What he couldn't ignore was the glint of tears and the trembling of her lower lip. He'd never been able to watch a woman cry.

He gave in. "When your uncle started working for me, we were looking for some very rare parts for an antique Mercedes a customer of mine was restoring. I'd exhausted my sources and was ready to give up the search, but then Quincy strolls in and lays the entire order of parts in front of me. When I asked where he'd gotten them, he said he knew a lot of mechanics in backwater towns and had managed to fill the order."

"That's why you think he's guilty?" Callie gasped. "Because he filled an order that you couldn't fill? He does know a lot of mechanics in backwater towns. It probably happened just like he said. He called them and they found the parts. If they were stolen, he didn't know it. Uncle Quincy trusts his friends. He'd never question their integrity."

"Callie, every time I ran into a snag getting rare parts, Quincy would show up with them within a week. That's about how long it would take to locate a rare car, steal it and break it down into parts. Besides, there's more."

Up to that point, Callie was convinced it was all a misunderstanding. When Ian announced there was more, his voice became gentle—it was the tone of voice used to prepare someone for really bad news.

Every tooth in Callie's mouth began to ache when he regarded her with sympathy. That look gave more veracity to his accusations than any words he could have spoken. For the first time in her life, she felt her faith in her uncle fade. She couldn't listen to what Ian had to say. Not now, anyway. Maybe not ever, because Quincy was the only person who'd remained steadfast in her life. The only person who'd ever put her first. The only one who'd ever really cared about her, stood beside her through the good and the bad, and there certainly had been more bad than good.

"We'll talk later," Callie said as she began to back down the hallway. "You must be freezing standing there in that towel, and you must be starving. Let's get you fed. Then we'll talk. Okay?"

"Sure," Ian murmured. Callie didn't hear him because she'd fled, unable to tolerate his horrible, sympathetic gaze for one more second.

In the kitchen, she turned on the faucet so the noise of running water would drown out the sound of her tears.

IAN'S EMOTIONS wavered between anger and self-pity. Anger—because he'd known Callie had been crying and had felt so sorry for her that he'd been stupid enough to let her go shopping for his clothes alone. Self-pity—because he'd trusted her to come back and after five hours it was apparent that she had no intention of returning.

A feeling of helplessness surged through him, and he slammed his fist against his thigh. He couldn't believe he was in this mess, and if he couldn't find Quincy, he was going to lose everything he'd worked so hard to build. How could he find Quincy without Callie's help? By now she'd probably found him and they'd gone into hiding. That left him with a one-way ticket up the river.

"It's just not fair," he muttered as he threw himself down on Callie's overstuffed sofa and rolled his eyes heavenward. "Do you hear me?" he yelled in frustration. "It's just not fair!"

"Well, you don't have to shout about it," Callie replied dryly as she came through the front door.

"You came back!" Ian exclaimed. He leaped to his feet so quickly that he slammed his shin against the edge of her mahogany coffee table. "Oh, damn! That hurt."

Callie laughed as she watched him lean down and rub gingerly at his abused leg. "Of course I came back. I told you I would."

"You've been gone forever."

"And you thought I'd deserted you." She gave him a disappointed shake of her head. "I said I'd help you, Ian. I *never* go back on my word."

Her tone remained light. Still, Ian recognized he'd just been chastised. "I guess I owe you an apology."

"Everyone's entitled to one mistake. Just don't repeat it."

"Are you always so forgiving?" he asked as she dropped several shopping bags on the sofa.

She looked up at him and smiled. Ian's stomach lurched. It was the first full smile she'd given him. For two cents, he'd pull her into his arms and kiss her until she couldn't breathe. Unfortunately he didn't have two cents. He'd given her all his money as a down payment on his loan. Should he call his father and ask him to wire him some money? No. He didn't want to involve his parents in this escapade unless he absolutely had to.

"Uncle Quincy always says that when you carry a grudge, you're just carrying excess baggage. I don't like excess baggage."

"To listen to you talk, you'd think Quincy was your father," he observed.

Her smile faded. "I went to live with him when I was thirteen, so I guess he is in a way." Clearly wanting to change the subject, she said, "Let's check out your new wardrobe."

Ian watched Callie as she began to remove her purchases—her expression as excited as that of a child handing out presents at Christmas.

He'd expected her to get him just the bare essentials: a few changes of underwear, a few simple shirts, a few pairs of jeans. All of that was there, but she'd also bought him a pair of dress slacks, a dress shirt and a light blue pullover. He picked up the sweater and looked quizzically in her direction. "It still gets cold in the evenings," she shyly explained. "Besides, the sweater's the same color as your eyes."

Her shyness surprised Ian. There was a hard edge to her—a constant message warning, "Hands off or you'll regret it." Yet she was genuinely shy, as well. It made her all the more intriguing.

His eyes roamed down her. The provocative red blouse she'd been wearing at the pool hall had been replaced by a simple white shirt, the skintight jeans by a navy blue skirt that was gathered at the waist and fell in soft folds to midcalf. The picture she presented right now blended perfectly with her apartment. He tilted his head and regarded her thoughtfully.

"If you don't like what I've chosen, I can take the clothes back," Callie declared defensively.

"The clothes are fine. I'm just wondering which woman is the real you."

"Which woman is the real me?" she repeated, confused.

He nodded. "Are you the outrageous Doc Watson or the demure Dr. Watson?"

Callie's heart gave a nervous little jump at the question, and she quickly glanced away. Folding up his clothes, she slowly responded, "They're both me."

"If you say so."

His agreeableness made her even more nervous. His tone indicated he didn't believe her. Suddenly she felt very exposed, very vulnerable. How had he picked up on one of her most scrupulously kept secrets? She realized then that she was going to have to be very careful around Ian Sherlock.

"Why were you gone so long?" Ian asked, sensing that he'd somehow pushed Callie into a corner. Now it was his turn to change the subject, though he would have preferred to continue questioning her on the nature of her two personalities.

"I had some bills to pay—the rent, phone and utilities. I also had to arrange to have my mail held, the newspaper stopped, and so on. I guess I should have called you but there was so much to do that I just didn't think about it."

"I'm sorry I've complicated your life," Ian said.

When she observed how apologetic he looked, she sighed heavily. She wanted to dislike him—given the fact that he was hell-bent on tossing her uncle into jail. But how could she dislike him when he was so guileless?

"My uncle got you into this mess in the first place, so I guess it's only fair that my life becomes a bit complicated." Before Ian could respond, she went on, "There's a small suitcase in the hall closet that you can use. While you pack, I'll fix dinner. If we're going to find Uncle Quincy, we need to get an early start tomorrow."

And then she was gone without having seemed to move. Ian was unable to identify the strange feelings coursing through him. They were as elusive as the woman.

The rattle of pots and pans got him off the sofa, and he went to the hall closet to retrieve the suitcase. When he lifted the sweater a short time later, her shy words came back to taunt him. *Besides, the sweater's the same color as your eyes.*

Who was the *real* Calandra Watson? Regardless of what she claimed, he knew one of them was a role. He wanted to believe that it was Doc Watson the pool hustler, but he couldn't quite convince himself that he was right.

CALLIE LIKED TO COOK, but it was a rare occasion when she was able to indulge herself in the kitchen. She ate most of her meals out. She found eating alone far too lonely in the first place, and downright depressing when she'd cooked the meal herself and didn't have anyone to compliment her on it. She spent more time watching Ian—who visibly was thoroughly relishing her beef Stroganoff and spinach salad—than eating herself.

He leaned back in his chair and let out a satisfied groan. "That was absolutely fabulous, Callie. What's for dessert?"

Callie eyed him in amusement. "You must have consumed three thousand calories. You can't possibly want dessert."

He looked crestfallen. "I always have dessert."

"There's a Danish in the refrigerator. Help yourself."

He was gone in a flash, and Callie smiled. When he returned, she once again watched him eat. He ate slowly savoring each morsel.

Callie finished her meal and pushed her plate away. She was surprised when Ian asked, "Why hasn't some lucky guy married you?"

"I could ask the same question," she replied.

He chuckled. "I'm not of that persuasion, Callie."

She grinned as she lifted her coffee cup to her lips. After taking a sip, she said, "I'm just not the marrying kind of woman. What's your excuse?"

Although there wasn't a ring on his finger, she knew that didn't mean the man was unencumbered. She was also curious about him. The more she knew about him, the better chance she'd have of saving Quincy's hide.

He shrugged. "I guess the right woman has never come along. There have been a few who've managed to strike some sparks. No one has ever really lit the fire. Do you know what I mean?"

"It sounds as if you're a romantic."

"Everyone is a romantic, even if they don't want to admit it. Come on, Callie, 'fess up," he teased as he settled his elbows on the table and cradled his chin in his hands. "Don't you secretly harbor a dream of Prince Charming bursting through your front door, sweeping you off your feet and living happily ever after?"

Callie shook her head. "I gave up on fairy tales when I was thirteen. Life isn't made up of romantic fantasies. It's made up of harsh realities. The sooner you face that fact, the sooner you're able to cope."

This time, it was Ian who sipped his coffee as he began to add two and two together. Callie had said she'd gone to live with Quincy when she was thirteen—the same age she'd given up her dreams. He wanted to ask what had happened that was so traumatic it would turn a kid into a cynic, but he didn't know her well enough to be that forward.

"Don't you consider yourself a Prince Charming?" she ribbed him.

He shrugged. "I suppose I would be for the right woman. You know, the one who would ignore the fact that I throw my dirty socks all over the house, that I tend to forget to take out the garbage and that I like to eat potato chips in bed."

Callie laughed. "It sounds as if you're looking for a domestic saint."

"Maybe. What's your idea of the ideal man?"

Callie mulled over his question as she finished her coffee. She'd long ago discovered that there was no such thing as an "ideal" man, and she had to give some thought to her answer.

"I guess he'd be honest and direct, without being cruel. He'd support me in my decisions, even if he thought I was wrong. And he'd always pick up his dirty socks, take out the garbage—and *never* eat in bed."

Ian burst into laughter. "And you think I'm looking for a saint?"

Callie found herself laughing along with him. It felt good to laugh. It had been a very long time since she'd done so, she realized with a pang.

"I'd better get these dishes into the dishwasher," she said, her wariness returning. She didn't like the spontaneity he seemed to bring out in her. Since she survived by her wits, every act she performed was carefully calculated—including laughter.

"Since you cooked, why don't you let me clean up?" he suggested.

"Absolutely not," she replied. "My idea of a perfect guest is one who stays out of my kitchen. You can watch television or if that doesn't appeal to you, I have a ton of books in my den. Feel free to help yourself."

Ian wasn't in the mood for watching television or reading, but he was becoming more curious about Callie by the minute. Roaming around her den might give him some insight into her. "Reading sounds good. Where's your den?"

"Right across from the guest room."

Moments later, Ian decided that when Callie had referred to her "den," she'd been using the term loosely. There were floor-to-ceiling bookcases on three of the four walls, and they were filled to overflowing. She had a small desk crammed into one corner. It was covered with a mountain of scientific books and papers—all of which seemed to deal with plants. But the room was dominated by a pool table, and its well-worn appearance indicated that it was the most-used item in the room.

Ian picked up one of the cues from the rack hanging on the wall, testing its weight and height. It was too light and too short, and he replaced it and lifted another. He'd nearly gone through the entire assortment of cues before he found one that felt right.

He was still testing it when Callie came in and leaned against the doorframe. "That's a sucker's cue," she informed him.

"A sucker's cue?"

"Uncle Quincy's term for a cue guaranteed to throw off your opponent's game."

Ian eyed the stick. "What's wrong with it?"

"It has a flat tip. If you want good English on the ball, you need a rounded, half-moon tip."

"So why do you have one with a flat tip?"

"For practice."

"Practice for what?"

"If you're working a hustle, you sometimes run into an amateur who really knows his game. In order to convince him that you're as inexperienced as you want him to believe you are, you pick out the worst cue in the joint. When you win, he thinks it was luck and you get out without a fight."

Ian leaned against the pool table, dropped the cue between his feet and rolled it between his hands. He felt stymied by all her contradictions—he couldn't connect the soft-looking woman in front of him with the outrageous woman he'd met at Kelly's this afternoon or, for that matter, with the infamous Doc Watson Quincy had told so many tales about.

"I just can't see you participating in a hustle," he said.

Callie grinned as she strolled into the room and took the cue away from him. "Hustling pool paid for my college education."

"So it was a means to an end?"

"Yes. But it's also fun."

"You enjoy cheating people?" Ian asked in astonishment.

Deeply offended by the accusation, she scowled at him. "I never cheat, Ian. I play the best game I can."

"But in a hustle, you make the other guy think you don't know what you're doing. No matter how you look at it, Callie, that's cheating."

She shook her head in disagreement. "I don't take his money out of his pocket. I don't slap it down on the table. He does that."

"He does it because you've challenged him."

"Sometimes. Most of the time he does it because he thinks he's found an easy mark. If cheating is the way you want to define it, then *he's* out to cheat *me*."

Ian took the cue away from her and put it back on the rack. "Even if that is true, you don't need to set them up. Most of the men I've met in pool halls are chauvinistic enough to believe that they can beat a woman— even if she is a pro—and it's obvious that you make every effort to use their preconceptions to your advantage."

"What in the world are you talking about?" Callie asked, baffled.

Ian gave her an admonishing look. "You don't just use your skill, you use your assets. You screw up his concentration by giving him an eyeful of your cleavage. Is winning so important to you that it's worth debasing yourself?"

"You don't know what you're talking about," she muttered as she spun angrily away from him.

He caught her arm and forced her to turn back and face him. "Hit a sore spot, did I?"

"You did not hit a sore spot!"

"Then why are you so mad?"

"I'm not mad!"

"No, you're furious. Are you furious at me or at yourself?"

She began to rub unconsciously at her jaw as she glared at him. He caught her hand, pulled it away from her face and held it against his chest. "Answer my question, Callie."

"You have a lot of nerve," she said through gritted teeth. "You come running into my life accusing my uncle of thievery. You ask me to help you find him so you can turn him over to the police. You borrow my money. You eat my food. You—"

"Answer my question, Callie."

"I will not!"

"Then I'll answer it for you," Ian countered, ignoring her murderous glare. "I don't think you like exposing your body to every Tom, Dick and Harry that wanders into Kelly's. All the same, there's a part of you that doubts your skill, so you have to cushion your odds, and the only way you know how to do that is to use what nature gave you. But even as you're using it, you're putting up a wall. You're saying, 'Look all you want, but don't touch.' I think you're afraid of being touched by a man."

"You don't know what you're talking about," she retorted.

"Don't I?"

Callie shivered as he tugged her hand up to his neck and pulled her against him. He was lean and hard and seductively masculine. What was even more seductive was the fact that even though there was desire in his eyes, his body remained relaxed.

Callie was an expert at resisting a physical threat, but she'd never been faced with an emotional one. That was precisely how she perceived Ian at that moment. He was attracted to her. She could see it in his eyes. Yet, he could control the emotion.

She found the unspoken challenge tantalizing. She relaxed against him until he was forced to wrap his arm around her waist to support her. Since he still gripped her one hand, she rubbed the other against his shoulder and then let it trail up into his hair. His muscles contracted beneath her fingertips but he still maintained control.

Her self-protective instincts warned her that she had to win this battle of wills—that it was imperative that she prove to Ian Sherlock right here and now that she called the shots.

She rose on tiptoe and brushed her lips against his, murmuring, "Is this the behavior of a woman afraid of being touched by a man?"

When he didn't respond, she kissed him again, this time more firmly. At first his lips were stiff. Then they

softened, parting slightly. Callie took immediate a
vantage by slipping her tongue inside.

She heard his low moan and deepened her kiss as s
moved her body against him, reveling in the new te
sion she felt in his coiled muscles and at his hardenir

She basked in the glory of her control. She wou
take him to the edge and then walk away. As far as s
was concerned, it was just punishment for his probi
into her personal life and making judgment calls in a
eas he knew nothing about.

But before she could achieve her revenge, Ian plac
his hands on her shoulders and thrust her away fro
him. When she peered up at him in confusion, he stat
tightly, "I make love, not war."

Before she could respond, he left the room, slar
ming the door behind him.

Shocked, she stared at the door. It was several mi
utes before she let herself admit that it wasn't his d
parture she found so unbelievable. It was the fact th
she'd actually enjoyed kissing him. And that realiz
tion scared her.

3

IAN GLANCED AT the digital clock beside his bed and sighed heavily. Time was crawling by. Was that what it would be like in prison? Minutes seeming like hours, hours seeming like days? He felt as if he'd been in bed for a week, and it wasn't even midnight.

He'd been lying there, staring up at the ceiling ever since he'd left Callie. More than once he'd cursed himself for not having had the foresight to grab a book on his way out. Not that he'd have been able to read after that little seduction scene in her den.

Ian had never been an advocate of self-torture, but he couldn't refrain from reliving those few moments he'd held her in his arms. He'd known she'd feel soft, but he hadn't realized how soft, or that her curves would mesh perfectly with the planes of his own body. He would have had to be a eunuch not to respond to her in the end.

He closed his eyes, recalling how her body had moved sinuously against his, how her lips had coaxed and her tongue had teased. He'd wanted to throw her on top of the pool table and make love to her. What had stopped him was his growing awareness that although she was thoroughly seducing him, she was completely detached.

That—more than anything—had him convinced that his assessment of her pool-hall demeanor was true: she used her body to gain the advantage.

His sexual thoughts drove him out of bed to stare out the window, which overlooked the parking lot. Callie had to be twenty-nine or thirty years old. Somewhere along the line she had to have met a man who'd been able to storm her defenses. Or maybe it was a man who'd caused her to put up those defenses in the first place.

Ian found the latter explanation more palatable—that Callie had had her heart broken and had decided to protect herself. He could understand that, having suffered through a few broken hearts himself. But he was far too gregarious to remain withdrawn for long. Besides, the way he had it figured, you had to suffer through a few broken hearts in order to recognize true love when it finally came along.

Oddly enough, his speculations about Callie relaxed him. He returned to bed, knowing that he'd now be able to sleep.

CALLIE had never suffered from insomnia till tonight. That it was Ian Sherlock's fault went without saying, and she was half tempted to stalk into the guest room and bop him over the head with the nearest heavy object.

Instead she finished cleaning out her refrigerator, disposing of all the perishables. When the chore was finally done, she went into the den, grabbed her cue and began to practice her trick shots.

Usually the activity relaxed her, but this time it only made her more agitated. Each shot she made evoked a memory of Quincy, who'd taught her everything she knew about pool. She desperately wanted to believe in her uncle's innocence, but couldn't forget Ian's change in demeanor as he started to give her the remainder of his evidence. What could her uncle possibly have done that would have Ian so firmly convinced that Quincy was the person who'd framed him?

It was quite possible Ian was guilty and was trying to place the blame on Quincy. She dismissed that idea almost as soon as it surfaced. She had no reason to believe that Ian was innocent, but believe it she did. She was also sure that if Quincy wasn't guilty, he knew who was. That meant she couldn't walk away from Ian if she wanted to. After their little scene in the den she fervently wanted to. But she knew what it was like to be in prison, and she wouldn't condemn an innocent man to even one hour of that horror.

She continued to practice her shots, mulling over ways to find Quincy. She could make a few phone calls, but if he'd put the word out that he was in hiding, his friends wouldn't reveal his whereabouts—not even to her. Her phone calls might turn this into a maddeningly elusive game of hide-and-seek. Considering the seriousness of Ian's dilemma, she couldn't let that happen.

Her only advantage was that money burned a hole in Quincy's pocket. In order for him to survive, he would never be far away from a pool parlor. She was sure he was frequenting those backwater towns he'd mentioned to Ian. She was also fairly certain which

ones they'd be, since she'd gone on the run with Quincy
on more occasions than she cared to remember.

As she watched her last ball drop into the pocket, she
recalled Quincy's message on the answering machine.
When she'd first listened to his nonsensical words, she'd
figured he'd gotten himself into a jam and had hefted a
few too many mugs of beer in an effort to console himself. But now she began to wonder if there wasn't a
hidden meaning in his message because she couldn't
remember him—even when he was ready to pass out—
ever spouting such nonsense.

She put her cue back on the rack and crossed to her
desk. There were no new messages on her answering
machine so Quincy's message would still be there. She
took out the cassette and dropped in a replacement.
After recording her standard announcement on the new
tape, she popped the old one into a portable cassette
player and leaned back in her chair to listen.

She grinned when her uncle's voice, shaded with a
lyrical Irish brogue, filled the room. She conjured up
his image.

At five foot seven and one hundred and forty
pounds, Quincy described himself as a welterweight.
His face was on par with Cary Grant's, right down to
the cleft in his chin. His graying head of night-black hair
added an air of impoverished gentry. His gift of gab was
positively larcenous and in a hustle he was absolutely
lethal.

Callie stopped the tape when his message came to an
end. After listening to it again, she was convinced
Quincy had been trying to tell her something. But
what? And why, if it was a secret message, had he felt

obliged to leave it in code? Had he known that Ian was looking for him and would eventually connect with her? Did Ian hold the key to unraveling the message?

She came to the conclusion that that was the only answer. Ian must know something that would shed some light on Quincy's message, and she had to know what it was.

She rewound the tape and hurried to the guest room, pausing long enough to give a quick knock before stepping inside. Ian was asleep, and she hesitated, wondering if it was really necessary to wake him. Her questions could wait until morning. But she was too eager to hear his answers, and she knew that she wouldn't be able to sleep until they'd talked.

"Ian?" she said softly as she walked to the edge of the bed.

His only response was to shift restlessly between the sheets.

"Ian?" she repeated. When he still didn't waken, she reached out and touched his bare shoulder, saying more loudly, "Ian, wake up."

She let out a small scream of surprise when he suddenly bolted upright. Before she knew what was happening, she was pinned to the mattress beneath his hard body.

"Ian, it's me. Callie!" she cried in alarm.

"What in hell are you doing in here?" He shook his head, as if trying to clear it.

"I need to talk to you," she replied weakly when he shifted, and she realized that not only was her skirt bundled around her waist, but Ian Sherlock was as naked as a newborn babe.

"You should have knocked first."

"I did. You didn't hear me."

He glanced toward the clock beside his bed. "No wonder I didn't hear you. I've only been asleep for an hour. Couldn't this conversation have waited until morning?"

Callie shook her head against the pillow, though she was really denying the press of his naked body and the flood of sensations it was creating inside her. She should have bought him some pajamas, she thought idly.

He mumbled what sounded like a curse, raised himself off her and tucked the sheet around his waist. "What's so urgent?"

"Uncle Quincy's message," she answered as she scrambled into a sitting position and readjusted her skirt. She blushed when she realized he'd been watching her.

"You woke me up to talk about the ravings of a drunken man?" he muttered irritably.

She pushed away the twinge of disappointment that arose at his disinterest in her. Now was not the time to develop a feminine ego. "I don't think they were the ravings of a drunken man. I think Uncle Quincy was trying to tell me something."

Ian looked doubtful but said, "Okay. What was he trying to tell you?"

"I don't know. But I think you do."

He eyed her askance. "Oh, come on, Callie. I'm under suspicion for grand theft auto. What would that have to do with finding the pot of gold at the end of the rainbow?"

"I don't know," she repeated, holding up her tape recorder. "Just listen to his message. Then tell me what you think."

Ian nodded. Callie hit the Play button on the recorder. Quincy's voice immediately filled the room.

Ah, colleen, it breaks my poor heart to be reduced to talking to a machine when I want to talk to you. But since I'm a man who's always loved the sound of his own voice, I suppose it's better to talk to a machine than not to talk at all. I've great news. I've finally found the end of the rainbow. Now, all I have to do is wrest the pot of gold away from the little people to prove to the world what I've always claimed: Quincy McKiernan was destined for greatness. Wish I could invite you along on the chase, but you know as well as I do how violently the little people react to crowds. This is a one-man hustle, but as soon as I've got my hands on the treasure, I'll give you a call. In the meantime, believe everything you hear about me, particularly if it's bad. After all, every man needs an unsavory reputation to live up to. Take care, Doc, and keep shooting the lights out.

"Well?" Callie prompted as she turned off the tape recorder.

"What does shooting the lights out mean?" Ian inquired.

Callie gave a dismissive wave of her hand. "That's just a saying in pool that means someone is shooting superbly. Did anything in his message mean anything to you?"

"Outside the fact that he said you should believe everything you hear about him—particularly if it's bad—nothing he said makes any sense to me," he stated dryly. "But what else is new? From what I can see, Quincy makes a career out of not making any sense."

Callie chewed on her bottom lip in frustration. She was still convinced that Quincy had been trying to tell her something, and she'd been certain Ian had the key to figuring out what it was. But if he didn't, then she did. But what in the world was it?

"Tell me what other evidence you have against Uncle Quincy," she said, needing all the facts in order to decide how to proceed from here.

Ian frowned, recalling her reaction this afternoon when he'd tried to give her all the details. Not only had she run but she'd ended up crying. He was desperate, but not so desperate that he wanted to break the woman's heart.

"Callie, I can assure you that my evidence has nothing to do with a rainbow, or a pot of gold, or even wresting it away from the little people."

"Ian, just tell me what it is."

He still hesitated, but he finally understood that she wasn't going to leave until she heard his answer. For a second he actually considered lying to her, but she'd only be hurt more in the end if he did so.

"One of my managers wanted to take an extended vacation. Lincoln Galloway's been with me from the beginning, Callie, and I trust him implicitly."

She nodded. "What does his vacation have to do with Uncle Quincy?"

Ian sighed and continued, "Quincy offered to cover for Lincoln, and he'd been doing such a good job, I agreed."

"And?" Callie prodded when he didn't go on.

"The salvage yard that Quincy took over is where the police found the chop shop."

Callie chewed on her thumbnail as she assimilated the information. "You're sure it wasn't there before Uncle Quincy took over?"

"It wasn't there, Callie. As I said, I trust Lincoln implicitly. Even if I hadn't, I made an inspection of the place before your uncle took over. No one could have hidden an operation of that magnitude from me."

Callie had her doubts about his last statement. She knew that Quincy could probably hide the White House from the president if he put his mind to it, but she didn't think Ian would be pleased to hear that, so she let his comment ride. "Do you have any more evidence?"

Ian shifted uncomfortably and tucked the sheet more tightly around his hips. "Each of my salvage yards has its own checking account. It makes it easier for my accountant to keep an accurate record of their business transactions. I was granted bail because my attorney got a handwriting expert to testify that my signature had been forged on a fortune's worth of checks made out to 'Cash.' All the checks were from Quincy's operation."

Callie buried her face in her hands. "I suppose Uncle Quincy had bragged about the fact that he was an expert at forging signatures?"

"You've got it."

Callie gave a miserable shake of her head. "I've seen him use that talent in a hustle. He'd bet someone that they couldn't identify their own signature from his facsimile of it, but it was always a game with him, Ian. I can't believe he'd actually forge your signature in order to commit a crime."

"That may be true, but how many people can actually forge a signature? I'd be hard-pressed to believe that I have two employees blessed with that talent."

"But it could happen."

"It's possible," he said, reluctant to lend any credence to her words, but she looked so hopeful that he knew he'd feel like an ogre if he disagreed. "But do you really think it's probable, Callie?"

"No." Callie sighed and rose from his bed. "You've just given me enough circumstantial evidence for me to suspect that even if you are guilty, Uncle Quincy is an accomplice. So why aren't the police searching for him?"

"Because when the police raided the chop shop, the people they caught pointed the finger at me as their leader. Also, I have no way to prove that the money from the forged checks was used in the car-theft operation. The district attorney pointed out that if Quincy did forge the checks, he could simply have been embezzling from me."

"But that still doesn't explain why they aren't looking for Uncle Quincy," Callie insisted with a troubled frown. "They should at least want to talk to him about the forged checks. And he was running the salvage yard for you—it would seem natural they'd want to question him to see if he'd known that the chop shop was there."

"I agree. But they already have half a dozen people ready to testify that I'm the brains of the operation, so why should they waste the taxpayers' money looking for Quincy? Plus, my attorney thinks the district attorney is holding something back."

"His sure shot into the pocket," Callie muttered.

"Or, as my attorney said, his ace in the hole. He thinks it might be a surprise witness whom they'll claim they kept secret to protect, I don't know why. I haven't been charged with a violent act to date. However, the way my luck's been running, I wouldn't be surprised if it happened tomorrow."

She paused in her pacing and eyed him thoughtfully. Quincy had mentioned how "violently" the little people reacted to crowds. Had he been trying to warn her? Or was his use of the word merely coincidental? "There haven't been any acts of violence? Not even threats?"

"Not that I know of."

"But you're not certain."

"Callie, right now the only thing I'm certain of is my own name."

"And your innocence."

He gave her a wry smile. "And my innocence."

"If there hasn't been any violence, then why would Uncle Quincy feel he had to leave a secret message?"

"Maybe it isn't a secret message. Maybe it really is the ravings of a drunken man."

She stopped at the window and leaned her head against the cool pane of glass. "No. I'm sure he was trying to tell me something. I just can't figure out what it is."

"Why don't you try sleeping on it?" Ian suggested, knowing that he had to get her out of the room. His body had been humming ever since he'd awakened enough to realize that Callie was lying beneath him, and he couldn't erase the feel of her from his mind. The temptation to sweep her into his arms and carry her back to bed was becoming too great, especially when she looked so woebegone. He wanted to offer her comfort in the most basic way, and he found that fact unnerving. He could understand his physical attraction to her, of course. He could also understand his curiosity about her. But where in the world were these feelings of protectiveness coming from? "Perhaps you'll wake up with the answer."

"Yeah." She pushed away from the window and moved toward the door. "I'm sorry I woke you."

She looked so defeated that Ian automatically responded. "Callie?"

She glanced over her shoulder at him and was momentarily stunned by the sight of him sitting up in bed with moonlight shimmering across his wide shoulders and bare chest. The subdued light seemed to delineate each and every one of his muscles, and she shivered at the memory of the hard length of him as he'd pressed her down into the softness of the mattress.

Longing—poignant and insistent—assailed her. Her knees began to shake. She reached for the door handle and gripped it. As she raised her gaze to his face, she saw her own needs reflected in his eyes. "Why are you doing this to me?" she asked plaintively.

Ian knew exactly what she was asking. He also knew that he could twist her question around so he wouldn't have to give her an honest answer. He could pretend that he misunderstood and reassert his claim that he was here because she was his only means to finding her uncle.

He could have lied but didn't. "This is as unexpected for me as it is for you. You aren't exactly the kind of woman I'm normally attracted to."

Her laugh was short and harsh. "And exactly what kind of woman am I, Mr. Sherlock?"

"A frightened one," he answered. "I just haven't figured out what you're frightened of. But I will."

"You're in no position to be making threats," she declared irritably.

"That wasn't a threat, Callie, and you know it. Why don't we call it a night?"

Callie wanted to argue with him. She didn't, however, because he was right. She was frightened. She'd only known Ian a few hours, but in those few hours she'd been able to determine that he was the type of man she used to dream about. He was kind. He was gentle. He was without artifice. He said he was attracted to her. But would he still feel that way if he knew that she had spent a year of her life in prison? She didn't think so. And that hurt her far more than she would ever have believed possible.

"Yes, Ian, it's time to call it a night," she replied wearily.

IT WAS BARELY SIX when Ian finished stowing the two
suitcases in Callie's car. She'd said she wanted to get an
early start, but he'd expected her to sleep in after her
wee-hours-of-the-morning visit with him. Instead, an
hour ago he'd awakened to the sound of the shower
running. He wondered if she'd gotten any sleep at all
last night.

He closed the trunk and leaned against the small Ford
while he waited for her. The sleepy town of King's
Creek was just starting to come to life, and Ian listened
to the crow of a rooster in the distance and the insistent
lowing of a cow needing to be milked. He'd grown so
used to the clamor of the city that the noises of the
country seemed foreign to him.

"You look pensive," Callie remarked when she joined
him.

Ian smiled. "I was just thinking about how quickly
we adapt. When I was a kid, I lived in the country and
woke up to the trill of a cardinal. Now I wake up to my
neighbor's teenage son starting his motorcycle. I miss
hearing the roar of his engine."

Callie laughed, and Ian decided he liked the way her
nose crinkled in mirth. Without thinking, he reached
out and trailed a finger down its length. Then he
touched the soft shadow beneath her right eye. "Did
you get any sleep?"

Callie glanced down at her feet and nervously jan-
gled her keys. "A little bit."

He hooked his thumb beneath her chin and raised her
head, forcing her to look at him. "I'm sorry, Callie," he
whispered, but he didn't know what he was apologiz-
ing for. All he knew was that she looked so darn sweet

standing there in baggy jeans and an oversize navy-blue sweatshirt that had King's Creek College emblazoned across the front of it in big gold letters.

"It's not your fault," she whispered back.

"I'm not so sure about that." His eyes traveled over her face, absorbing each plane and hollow. "I want to kiss you."

His words vibrated through Callie. What harm could possibly come from one small kiss? "So what's stopping you?"

It was the response Ian wanted to hear, and he pulled her into his arms. He watched her lips part slightly in anticipation, and he trailed his fingers along her jaw before stroking her bottom lip with his thumb.

Callie shook at the provocative gesture and tentatively touched the tip of her tongue to his thumb. She was rewarded by his groan of approval, and then he sealed his lips over hers.

The warmth of his mouth pervaded her, melting away four years' worth of frost. The stroke of his hands over her body was like a gentle rain against parched earth. She was starving for sustenance, and he was nourishing her. She wrapped her arms around his neck and clung to him.

Ian had been unprepared for her ardent response— it shocked and aroused him. He couldn't have pulled away from the kiss if he'd wanted to. Heaven help him, he didn't want to.

You're playing with fire. Her allegiance lies with her uncle, and she'll do anything to protect him. His self-protective instincts were checked—at least for now— by his libido.

Yesterday she'd kissed him with finesse, but hadn't responded. Now she was responding, but her kiss was as unpolished as a neophyte's. Ian found her lack of skill far more exciting because he knew he was kissing the shy Dr. Watson, not the flamboyant Doc Watson. He definitely preferred the former woman.

A door slammed close by and Callie jumped away from him as if scalded. Ian reluctantly released his hold on her and smiled as he watched an embarrassed blush brighten her cheeks.

"I, uh, think we'd better get on the road," she stammered, once again looking down at her feet.

"I suppose we should," Ian said, straining to sound casual. "Where do we go from here?"

Callie's head shot up and she frowned at him, knowing that his question didn't relate to destination. "I can't get involved with you."

"Why not?" When she didn't answer, he asked, "Is it because I'm a wanted man?"

She gave a wretched shake of her head. "It has nothing to do with you."

There were a thousand questions bouncing around inside Ian's head, but he didn't ask any of them. He had to get his priorities in order. His first priority was finding Quincy so he could prove his innocence. When he'd accomplished that task, then he could concentrate on solving the mystery of Dr. Calandra Watson, botanist and pool hustler.

He took the keys from her hand. "I think I'd better drive. I had more sleep than you did."

Callie wasn't in any shape to drive, but her condition had nothing to do with a lack of sleep. She was still trembling from Ian's kiss, and it was going to be a long time before she recovered. For the past four years, she'd been struggling to find her place in the world. She'd finally come to grips with the understanding that you *were* what you were born to be, and no amount of dreaming or hard work was going to change that. Ian was rocking the very foundations of that belief. He was making her dream again—want again. And he had no right to do that.

"Leave me alone."

She didn't realize she'd spoken aloud until Ian said, "I'd have a better chance of convincing the moon not to hang out with the stars." When she looked at him, her expression was angry and her eyes bleak. Ian smoothed his hand against her hair. "Whatever it is, Callie, we'll work it out."

She jerked away from his touch. "If you want to find Uncle Quincy, then we'd better stop dawdling and get this show on the road."

Ian's temper flared at her curt words. He forced himself to hold it in check, instinctively knowing that yelling at Callie would only make her withdraw further. He drew in a deep breath and released it to a slow count of ten. By the time he'd finished, Callie had gotten into the car and was waiting for him. When he started to climb inside, he saw a white envelope lying on the driver's seat with Callie's name written across it in a bold scrawl that looked terribly familiar.

He glanced toward Callie, who was staring out her window, her posture indicating that she had every intention of ignoring him.

"Callie, either your mailman has a unique way of delivering the mail, or someone was in your car last night."

Callie turned her head toward him. "What are you talking about?"

Ian looked down at the seat, and Callie followed his gaze. She grimaced as she reached for the envelope.

"It's from Quincy, isn't it?" Ian asked when she lifted it.

Callie nodded, feeling numb as she stared at her name. She'd recognize Quincy's handwriting anywhere. He'd been here last night. Why hadn't he come to her apartment? Unless, of course, he'd known that Ian was with her. But how could he have found that out?

By calling Kelly's, she realized. Mick was overprotective of her. If Quincy had called, he would have told him about the "gent" who'd come looking for Doc and left with her. Her wisdom tooth started to throb and she rubbed at her jaw as she stared at the envelope. Whatever was inside was bad news.

"Don't you think you should open it?" Ian asked as he got into the car and shut the door.

Callie nodded again. She turned the envelope over, amazed to see that her hands weren't shaking when she was trembling so badly inside.

Anxious to know what Quincy had written, Ian had to grip the steering wheel to keep from grabbing the envelope away from her and ripping it open. It seemed to take her forever to open the flap, and he held his breath in anticipation as she removed a single sheet of paper and unfolded it.

Callie couldn't believe what she was reading. So she read the note a second time.

Callie,
I've just learned that you've joined forces with Ian Sherlock. By doing so, you've betrayed me, and that leaves me with only one option. I'll be reporting you to the police at six-thirty this morning, and we both know how the cops will react to the news that you're involved with a wanted man. Was helping him worth losing your freedom? I think not, but you'll have a long time in a prison cell to think about it, won't you?

Quincy

"Callie, what is it?" Ian asked with concern as he watched the color begin to drain from her face.

She crumpled the note in her hand until it was enclosed in a white-knuckled fist. Her eyes glowing with fury, she glanced up at Ian. "We have to get out of here. Uncle Quincy is turning us in to the police," she told him, her voice deadly calm.

4

IAN WAS SO STAGGERED by Callie's announcement that he could only look at her in astonishment. Eventually he spoke. "He can't turn us in to the police. You're his niece!"

"What does that have to do with anything?" she shot back.

"It has everything to do with anything," Ian said reproachfully. "People don't turn members of their family in to the police when they haven't done anything wrong."

"You're *such* an innocent, aren't you?" she remarked sarcastically. She held up a hand to silence him. "We can discuss this matter later, Ian. Right now, we have to get out of here."

"No. I'm the one the police are after, so I'll leave. I'm not about to get you into trouble," Ian stated.

Callie regarded him with grim amusement. What would he say if she told him that she was already in trouble for violating her parole by becoming involved with a bail jumper. She had no intention, however, of enlightening him. Well, if she was going back to prison anyway, she was going to make the trip worthwhile. Quincy had threatened to take away her freedom. When she found him—and she would find him—she was going to exact her pound of flesh.

"I have to go with you, Ian. If I don't, you'll never find Uncle Quincy."

"I'll find him. Just tell me how to look for him." His lips settled into an unyielding line.

"Telling you how to find him won't do you any good," Callie replied with strained patience. "I'm a pool hustler—a member of the club. You haven't got a chance without me because no one is going to talk to you."

Callie was only repeating his own conclusions from yesterday, and he felt frustrated. He was certain he wouldn't find Quincy without her help. Yet if he did involve her, she was going to be in trouble with the police. However, once he cleared his name, she'd be cleared, so it was okay to accept her help. But what would happen to her if he was unable to clear his name?

She laid her hand on his arm and said persuasively, "I want to help you, Ian, but the only way I can do that is to go with you. I understand the risks involved, and I'm willing to take them. Once we find Uncle Quincy, you act on your knight-in-shining-armor inclinations and rescue damsels in distress to your heart's desire."

"Why are you so damn cynical?" he snapped. She was treating him as if he were some babe in the woods instead of a man with thirty-five years of well-earned life experience under his belt.

"Because I'm a realist." She glanced down at her watch. "Uncle Quincy said he'd be calling the police at six-thirty. Luckily we got an early start this morning, so if we hurry, we can avoid them."

"Why would Quincy warn you that he was contacting the police?" Ian asked, trying to understand her uncle's strange behavior. He was good at reading people. He couldn't believe that he'd misread Quincy this badly. Sure, he could see him breaking the law, but he would have sworn that the man was loyal to the people he cared for. Ian had never doubted that Quincy cared for Doc Watson. That was why he'd gone looking for Doc in the first place. Something was wrong here. Terribly wrong. And Ian didn't like it.

"I suppose he did it out of a sense of fair play," Callie answered with a dismissive shrug. She had too many other problems to deal with at the moment—such as planning their escape—to worry about Quincy's motives. "We're going to have to ditch my car. Lucy will loan me hers, so transportation won't be a problem. We're also going to have to hit the automatic teller at my bank. I can only withdraw three hundred dollars at one shot. After today, the police will be watching my bank account. If we don't find Uncle Quincy in a week or two, then we'll have to supplement our income by hustling pool."

Ian stared at her in dismay. There was an excited gleam in her eyes that he found disturbing. He'd almost swear that she was looking forward to going on the run!

His gut instincts insisted that there was much more going on than was apparent on the surface. For his safety and Callie's, he'd better get to the bottom of the matter as soon as possible. Bad enough, making Callie a fugitive from the law; worse still, becoming a player in a game he didn't understand.

His questions would have to wait. If Quincy intended to carry out his threat, they didn't have time to waste. He turned the key in the ignition and asked Callie for directions.

QUINCY COULDN'T STAND the confinement of his motel room one moment longer. Though he knew he was taking a risk, he ordered Devon to meet him at the coffee shop down the street.

When his friend came in, Quincy cursed. Devon was wearing a trench coat and a low-brimmed hat and couldn't have looked more conspicuous if he'd walked in stark-naked. A dozen pairs of eyes followed him as he walked to Quincy's booth. Quincy cursed again. He was going to have to find another hideout because there were now a dozen people who could identify him—all of them looking like they'd sell out their mother for a six-pack of beer.

"Devon, why are you dressed like that?" Quincy rasped when his friend joined him.

Devon grinned. "I'm dressed for danger."

Quincy sighed. "You've also called attention to us. I'm going to have to find a new hideout. Don't you have any sense?"

"You're the one who left your lair, so don't impugn my intelligence," Devon stated. "I told you that telephone communication should be our chosen modus operandi when chronicling my observations."

"My word, you're getting worse!" Quincy said sharply. "What happened to Callie? Did the police pick her up?"

"She avoided apprehension," Devon informed him.

"She got away?" Quincy gasped in horror.

When Devon nodded, Quincy banged the table with his fist. Why had he warned her that he was going to call the police? Why hadn't he just called them and forgotten about it? Because an integral part of him rebelled at turning Callie in without giving her a chance to escape.

Quincy dragged a hand across his face as he asked, "I don't suppose she left Ian Sherlock behind."

"Your supposition is sound."

"Take off that ridiculous hat and coat so we can get out of here," Quincy ordered. "We have to find a new place for me to hide."

"CALLIE! I wasn't expecting to see you until next week," Lucy Coates said, surprised when Callie strolled into the office of Coates Landscaping Service.

Callie hugged her friend and part-time employer. "I know, but I need to borrow your car. Uncle Quincy's in trouble, and the rat has the police looking for me."

"Oh, no!" Lucy's pleasantly plump, middle-aged face screwed up in an expression of exasperation as she pulled away from Callie's embrace. "Is that man ever going to grow up?"

"You tell me," Callie replied. "You've known him longer than I have."

"Don't remind me," Lucy grumbled. Then her brown eyes lit with interest as they landed on Ian. "Who's the hunk?"

"Uncle Quincy's latest victim," Callie explained. "Lucy, this is Ian Sherlock. Ian, Lucy Coates."

"I'm glad to meet you," Ian responded politely while eyeing the woman curiously. She was one of the short-

est and roundest women he'd ever seen. Her red hen-
naed hair clashed dramatically with her purple
coveralls. Despite her bizarre appearance, Ian was impressed by her sweet disposition and by the evident affection she had for Callie. He knew he'd like Lucy
Coates.

"You don't look like a stick. How in the world did you
get involved with Quincy?"

"A stick?" Ian repeated in confusion.

"That's a regular player in a pool parlor," Callie told
him with a chuckle.

"Oh," Ian mumbled, chagrined that Callie was already proving how lost he was in her world—reaffirm-
ing that without her, his chances of finding Quincy
were next to none.

Lucy laughed. "I have a feeling that this is a story I
want to hear."

"And I'll give you every nitty-gritty detail as soon as
I've found Uncle Quincy," Callie promised. "Ian and I
need to get out of town as soon as possible. Can you
ditch my car?"

"Sure," Lucy answered. "Will the police be contacting me?"

"Probably. You are my employer of record."

Lucy sighed in resignation. "Well, you know me. My
memory is a hairbreadth long. Were you here last
Wednesday, or was it last Thursday? Do you want me
to water your plants, check out your place while you're
gone?"

"Thanks, Lucy. I owe you," Callie said, hugging the
woman again.

"You just take care. When you get hold of Quincy, you tell him that this time he's going to answer to me," Lucy responded, returning the hug.

"I want to bring him back, not send him running for the hills," Callie quipped.

"Only the threat of marriage would send Quincy running for the hills. Otherwise he's fearless. You know where my car keys are. While you get them, I'll entertain Ian," Lucy declared.

Reluctant to leave Ian with Lucy, Callie hesitated. Ian was too inquisitive, and Lucy too talkative. She'd be leaving them alone for *only* a couple of minutes. They couldn't share *that* much information about her in such a short time, she assured herself as she headed for the back room.

The moment Callie disappeared through the doorway, Lucy turned toward Ian, worried concern etched on her face. "Whatever Quincy's done is serious, isn't it?" she asked.

"Yeah," Ian replied.

"Look after Callie, Ian. She isn't as tough as she thinks she is."

"You could have fooled me," he muttered.

"That's the problem. She fools herself," Lucy stated emphatically. "I wish—" She stopped. "Never mind. Promise me that you'll look after her."

"I'll do my best," Ian said, his gaze drifting to Callie as she came back into the room. Their eyes met. He felt a stirring of tenderness and a resurgence of the protective feelings he'd had last night.

He told himself that feeling protective of the hard-as-nails Doc Watson was ridiculous. He then recalled that wonderful, shy kiss they'd shared this morning. Again he was baffled by her Jekyll-Hyde personality. Which one was the real woman?

Callie stopped in the doorway. Her mouth went dry when she saw how intently Ian was regarding her. It was crazy, but she felt as if he were laying claim to her.

The thought was ridiculous. Even if she wanted to become involved with Ian Sherlock, she couldn't. A nun and a hooker would have more in common than they did. What would happen when he learned the truth about her? She refused to think about that. It was too depressing.

"We'd better get out of here," she said softly, unable to drag her gaze away from his.

"Yeah," Ian murmured, his voice sounding gruff.

"Happy hunting! Don't do anything I wouldn't do," Lucy told them with a laugh.

Callie shot her friend a warning look. Lucy innocently grinned back at her. Lucy's smile rattled Callie more than Ian's look had. Why?

Later, she promised herself, she'd figure out why. In fact, the moment she was sure she and Ian were safe, she'd sit down and think this entire situation through—including Quincy's traitorous behavior.

IAN SURREPTITIOUSLY cast a side glance at Callie. They were traveling down a deserted country road that ran along the border between Pennsylvania and Maryland. She was curled up in the passenger seat, her eyes glued to the windshield. Apart from a few directions, she hadn't said a word, and Ian had been reluctant to interrupt her thoughts. But as the odometer ticked off another mile, he knew he couldn't maintain his silence any longer. He had too many questions that needed answers.

"You work for Lucy?" he asked, starting with the innocuous in order to work up to the more important issues.

Callie swung her head toward him. "Whenever she needs help. Landscaping is seasonal. So it's either feast or famine."

"Having a doctorate in botany must be very useful in landscaping."

"Not really." Callie adjusted her seat belt so she could lean against the door and face him. "All you need to know is what plants are indigenous to the area and their growth cycles. After that, it's no more than a matter of figuring out which combinations are pleasing to the eye and how much work a client is willing to devote to caring for them."

"You make it sound easy."

"It *is* easy."

"So where's the challenge?"

"What makes you think I need a challenge?"

Ian returned his attention to the road. Callie had the impression that during their exchange he'd analyzed her right down to the tips of her toes. Her self-protective instincts went on red alert.

"Well?" she prodded when he didn't answer her question.

"Getting a Ph.D. takes a lot of hard work," he said. "You don't do it just for the fun of it. You do it because you have a specific goal in mind. Goals are challenges, Callie. Why did you walk away from yours?"

"Maybe my goal was simply the self-satisfaction of proving I could earn a Ph.D.," Callie suggested, quaking inside. Again, he'd picked up on one of her most scrupulously kept secrets. How did he manage to do that?

"Maybe," he murmured. However, the sardonic smile he gave her implied he didn't believe her. Before Callie could decide whether or not it would be productive to argue with him, he asked, "What's Lucy's relationship with Quincy?"

"What makes you think they have a relationship?"

Ian laughed. "It's a simple matter of adding two and two. You told Lucy that she'd known Quincy longer than you have. Her comments about him demonstrated more than a passing acquaintance with him. There was also a fondness in her voice when she talked about him. I'd hazard that at some time they were intimately involved."

"That's pretty good, Sherlock," Callie replied, relaxing now that the conversation had veered away from her. "As a matter of fact, Uncle Quincy and Lucy have known each other since childhood, and they've been engaged for twenty years."

"You're kidding me!" Ian exclaimed.

"Watch the road," Callie warned with a soft laugh, inordinately pleased at having been able to surprise him. It proved that the man wasn't infallible in his insight into people. Maybe he wasn't as big a threat as she'd perceived him to be.

Ian frowned. "Why would a woman waste twenty years of her life waiting for a man to marry her? You'd think she'd have taken the hint years ago that his intentions weren't honorable."

"But Uncle Quincy's intentions *are* honorable," Callie said in defense of her uncle.

Ian gave her a skeptical look. "Oh, come on, Callie. An honorable man would either have married Lucy or let her go. He wouldn't let her sit around for twenty years waiting for a marriage that's never going to happen."

"As a matter of fact, Uncle Quincy has offered Lucy her freedom on a regular basis, but she's refused every time."

"That's an easy out for Quincy," Ian muttered disgruntledly. "If he was really offering her her freedom, he would have told her it was over. Then he would have stayed away from her so she'd be forced to get on with her life. He hasn't done that, has he?"

"He's tried. But he loves Lucy."

"Then why hasn't he married her?"

"Because he's a pool hustler," Callie answered. "He thrives on the thrill of pitting himself against a good player. When he's finally managed to beat everyone of any consequence in an area, he gets the itch to move on. It's an itch he can't resist. He believes it isn't the type of life to subject a wife to."

"But he never thought twice about subjecting his niece to it, did he?" Ian said disapprovingly.

"My situation was different," she responded stiffly. "Uncle Quincy got stuck with me. It wasn't a matter of choice."

Ian's laugh was mirthless. "A man becomes responsible for a thirteen-year-old kid. Instead of settling down and giving her a home, he hauls her through pool halls and turns her into a hustler. He had a choice, Callie. He just didn't choose to select the right one."

"Don't pass judgment on things you know nothing about!" Callie snapped.

Ian knew he'd just hit on a sore spot and he pulled the car to the side of the road. After switching off the ignition, he turned toward her and demanded, "Then give me the facts so I can make an informed judgment."

"The facts are none of your business! We don't have time to sit and chat. The police could catch up with us at any minute," she sniped. Ian had already proven that he was far too perceptive. It would be a big mistake to start telling him personal details of her life. It might start out innocently enough with her childhood, but then he'd begin asking about her adulthood.

Callie wasn't sure why she was determined to hide her more recent past from him. It certainly wasn't a secret. In fact, just about everyone knew about her criminal record. She figured that Ian would either react to the news with disgust or pity—she abhorred both emotions, especially when they were directed at her.

Ian surveyed the road, noting that it was surrounded by dense woods. "I doubt there's been a police officer on this road in years. There isn't enough traffic to warrant setting up a speed trap. I think we're safe."

Callie glared at him. Ian smiled as he released his seat belt and shifted into a more comfortable sitting position. When he crossed his arms over his chest, it was obvious he was settling in for the duration.

"My life story doesn't have anything to do with your search for Uncle Quincy," she objected after several minutes of silence.

"I think it has a lot to do with my search for Quincy," he rebutted. "You're angry with him for turning us in to the police. Anger makes people do stupid things. Since I'm placing my life in your hands, it's only fair that I understand your relationship with your uncle. That way, if I see you doing something foolish, I can point it out to you."

"My relationship with Uncle Quincy will not cloud my judgment!" Callie argued vehemently.

"And I say you're too close to him to be objective!" Ian argued back just as vehemently. "Why did you go to live with Quincy when you were a kid?"

It had been years since Callie had even allowed herself to think about the past. She closed her eyes against all her painful memories. But the action didn't shut them out. It only made them more vivid. Suddenly she felt claustrophobic. She opened her eyes, released her seat belt and climbed out of the car, needing a deep breath of fresh air.

How much should she tell him? Well, she might as well give him the whole unvarnished truth about her childhood. Then maybe he'd leave her be and wouldn't push for details about her adulthood.

"What was your childhood like? Average or above average? Rich or poor?" she asked, glancing up at him when he joined her.

Ian shrugged. "Average, I guess. My parents are retired now. My father was a mechanic, my mother, a legal secretary. We didn't have a lot of money, but we had enough to afford the comforts of a middle-class family."

She walked to the side of the road and plucked a dandelion blossom. She twirled it between her fingers. "*Taraxacum officinale.* Did you know that that's the scientific name for the common dandelion?"

"No," Ian said as he stared at her inscrutable features, trying to anticipate where their conversation was heading.

"It's quite a plant, when you think about it," she continued as she studied the blossom. "You can make dandelion wine from it. The milky juices of its roots have medicinal value. You can eat its greens. Bees make honey from its nectar, and birds eat its seeds. But despite all its uses, people consider it a pesky, unsightly weed. It's mowed down, dug up and sprayed. Still, it manages to thrive."

"So what's the moral?" Ian asked.

"People like me and Uncle Quincy are like the dandelion," Callie replied, raising the blossom to her nose and inhaling its fragrance. "Despite the odds, we survive and make our contribution to society in our own inimitable way. If nothing else, people can point us out to their children and say, 'That isn't what you want to be when you grow up.'"

"Don't you think you're being too hard on yourself?"

"No. I think I'm being realistic." When Ian looked skeptical, Callie added, "Once upon a time there was a young woman named Jillian. She was very pretty and idealistic. Sure, she'd grown up on the wrong side of the tracks, but she didn't let that get her down. She knew

that someday Prince Charming would ride up on his
white charger, scoop her up into his arms and carry her
off to live happily ever after."

"Jillian is your mother," Ian guessed.

"How did you figure that out so quickly?" Callie
questioned with reluctant admiration.

"I've asked about your childhood. You don't strike
me as a woman who'd use an alias to tell her story."
When she didn't respond, he prodded, "Since you're
here to tell me the story, I assume Prince Charming
showed up."

"In a manner of speaking," Callie answered. "Except he wasn't riding a white charger—he was driving
a red sports car. He did scoop her up into his arms.
Then, when she popped up pregnant, he handed her
some money, suggested an abortion and hit the gas
pedal. You can still see the skid marks from his tires to
this very day."

"I'm sorry, Callie," Ian murmured sympathetically.

"I don't want your pity."

"Fine. I won't give it."

"Good." She tossed the dandelion to the ground and
nudged at it with the toe of her sneaker. "My mother
refused to believe that my father had left her hanging
high and dry. She was convinced he'd be back and the
three of us would be one big happy family. But she
eventually had to face the truth, and couldn't deal with
it. She began to find her consolation in the bottom of a
bottle.

"But drinking is an expensive habit, and waiting tables doesn't pay that well," Callie went on. "She was
still pretty, though, and she discovered the men would

gladly provide the bottle. All she had to do in return was sleep with them."

Ian resisted the urge to comfort her when she started massaging her temples as if trying to alleviate a pounding headache. He sensed she'd consider any gesture he offered as pity. He supposed she'd be right. It was impossible not to feel sorry for her. However, it wasn't just pity stirring inside him; the protective feelings were back stronger than ever.

"You know," she stated bluntly, "I wish my mother had been a hooker."

"You don't mean that, Callie," he gently chided.

"Yes, I do." She raised her head, her eyes bleak. "At least she'd have been using her body for profit. As disreputable as prostitution is, it's still more honorable than being the town floozy. You don't know what it's like to walk down the street and have people snicker at you because your mother is a drunken joke. You don't know what it's like to see her drag in anything in pants, so roaring drunk that she doesn't even remember the man's name the next day—assuming, of course, that she'd bothered to ask for it in the first place. You don't know what it's like to be thirteen and have—" She stopped abruptly. "I think you get the picture."

"What happened when you were thirteen?" Ian pressed.

She scowled at him, her chin tilted defiantly. For a long moment, Ian didn't think she was going to answer, but eventually she said, "One of my mother's 'friends' decided that I was a tempting morsel, and when she passed out, he came after me."

"He raped you?" Ian gasped in horror.

"No," Callie replied. "Luck was on my side. Uncle Quincy showed up for an unexpected visit. He tossed the bum out, packed my bags and took me with him because my mother refused to get help for her drinking problem—even after she learned what had just happened to me.

"The life Uncle Quincy provided me with might be unsavory to you," she opined, "but it was far better than the one I'd had for thirteen years. So don't *ever* criticize him for that."

Quincy may have provided her with a better life than her mother had, but Ian felt the man would have performed a far better service if he'd settled down with Lucy and given Callie a home. The belligerent look on her face informed him that his views on the matter weren't welcome, so he decided to keep them to himself.

Now that Ian knew Callie's story, he did have a clearer understanding of what motivated her. Except for one thing—why was she hustling pool instead of using her Ph.D.? He knew for certain that she hadn't gotten the degree for the satisfaction of proving she could do it. She had the kind of background that would make her struggle to be an upstanding member of society, and the best way to accomplish that was through education. In fact, he'd wager that getting her doctorate had become an obsession. So what had happened to change all that?

He really wanted to press the issue, but he knew that he'd already dragged more out of Callie than she'd been willing to give. "Well, I suppose we'd better get back on the road."

That was it? Callie thought. He'd just coerced her into telling him about her sordid childhood, and he wasn't even going to comment on it?

Callie realized she was being contrary. She hadn't expected Ian to judge her based on her mother's actions. She'd spent enough time with him to know that he wasn't the type of man who'd proclaim "Like mother, like daughter." She had, however, expected to hear him repeat the well-meaning platitudes that nice people always gave in response to the story of her life.

When he smiled broadly as he opened the car door, she eyed him with suspicion. As she slid into the car, she resolved that from this moment on she wouldn't let her guard down for one moment. Ian Sherlock was too sharp. She'd given him as much about her past as she was going to give him. She wouldn't answer any more of his questions. Not one.

When Ian climbed into the car, he blew her vow right out of the water by asking, "Where's your mother now?"

"She died last year," Callie answered dully. "Nearly thirty years of booze took their toll."

Ian didn't say a word. He reached over and drew her into his arms. Callie told herself that she wasn't going to cry as she rested her head against his shoulder. She didn't, though her chest ached with the need to do so.

"You loved her," he whispered against her hair.

"Of course I loved her," Callie whispered back. "She was my mother."

Ian's heart contracted at her confession. Did she realize just how terribly vulnerable she was?

No, she didn't, he decided a moment later. He suspected that she'd built up so many protective walls over the years that she probably didn't know what she was feeling half the time. Suddenly he understood that Quincy was all she had. Even if Quincy had framed him, he'd do everything he could to keep the man from going to prison. Callie *needed* Quincy. He was going to make sure that for once in her life she got what she needed.

5

IAN GRIMACED when he stepped into his motel room. He would never have believed the interior could look worse than the exterior. He went over to the bed, lifted the covers and was relieved to see that at least the sheets were clean. Hopefully the bathroom would also meet minimum health standards.

"Looking for bedbugs?" Callie asked.

Ian spun around to find her standing in the open doorway. "More like psychopaths. Are you sure this isn't the Bates Motel?"

Callie laughed and strolled into the room, her hands tucked into the front pockets of her baggy jeans. "Come to think of it, the desk clerk did have a passing resemblance to Anthony Perkins. You'd better keep an eye out when you take a shower."

"I'll do that." He frowned at her. "Is it really necessary to stay here when there's a perfectly decent motel right down the road?"

"It's necessary." Since there were no chairs in the room, Callie sat on the foot of his bed. "In the first place, our cash flow is limited, and we can get two rooms here for half the price of one there. Secondly, this is the type of place Uncle Quincy would stay in. In the evening, I'll do a little discreet questioning of our neighbors to see if anyone has seen him. A good many

of them live here year-round, so they would have noticed a stranger."

Ian recalled the "neighbor" he'd seen entering a room
when they arrived—if the man wasn't a potential mur-
derer, he would eat his loafers. He knew he shouldn't
let her rub elbows with the dregs holed up in this re-
volting place. If he opened his mouth, though, he knew
Callie would only accuse him of playing knight in
shining armor again.

"Why do you have to question the neighbors? Why
don't you just talk to the desk clerk?" he asked.

"That's elemental, Sherlock," she replied, her eyes
brightening with a glint of laughter. She was treating
him like a babe in the woods again, which annoyed
him.

It didn't matter if Callie viewed him as some innocent with no sense of the harsh realities—he knew who
and what he was. "What's 'elemental'?" he casually
asked.

"Desk clerks in motels like these are larcenous to the
core," she explained. "I'd have to bribe him for information. The clerk would probably say he hadn't seen
Uncle Quincy, whether he was here or not. Then the
minute I was gone, he'd contact Uncle Quincy and tell
him that for a price, he'd keep his mouth shut. Uncle
Quincy would pay him and skip. The moment he was
gone, the clerk would come running to me and say that
for another couple of bucks, he'd take me to Uncle
Quincy's room. Of course, he'd be horrified when we
found that Uncle Quincy had split. Finally, since he'd
given me the information in good faith, I'd be obliged
to let him keep his bribe."

Ian's annoyance increased while listening to her. She spoke with such certainty about a scenario he'd heretofore assumed only occurred in bad movies. Her eyes were lit with that damn excited gleam again. She was enjoying this trip into the realm of B movies!

"How are you going to go about conducting this discreet questioning?" he asked.

"Cautiously," she replied with a vague wave of her hand. She rose to her feet and stuffed her hands back into her pockets. "We have some time before we start looking for Uncle Quincy. Want to go for a walk?"

He cast a disparaging look around his room before giving her a wry smile. "Considering my alternative, what do you think?"

She grinned and shook her head. "Get your key, Sherlock."

"It's already in my pocket," he said as he pushed himself away from the wall. "Lead the way."

Outside, Callie turned the way leading out of town. They ambled down the country road in companionable silence for several minutes, enjoying the sunshine and the flower-scented spring breeze. When they began to follow a dirt side-road winding its way between two large apple orchards, Ian asked, "Why did you decide to go into botany?"

She smiled. "I've always loved living things. Why did you go into auto salvage?"

"As I said before, my father was a mechanic, and he used to say that if he had any sense, he'd quit getting his hands dirty and sell parts because that's where the real money was. By the time I started college, I knew I wanted to be my own boss, so I got a degree in business administration. After I graduated, a friend of my father's told me about an auto-salvage yard that was up for sale. I bought it through a little creative financing."

"You said you own a chain of auto-salvage yards. How many are there?"

"Six. I was in the process of buying number seven when this mess started." He sighed. "The deal fell through. I don't know if it'll still be on the market when I finally get everything straightened out."

"I'm sorry, Ian," Callie murmured sympathetically.

He gave a philosophical shrug. "As my mother says, everything happens for a reason. If it's meant to be, then it's meant to be."

Callie supposed that was as good a philosophy to live by as any. She really couldn't think of one reason for most of the events that had taken place in her life, though. Refusing to succumb to her maudlin mood, she changed the subject. "Do you have any brothers or sisters?"

"An older brother and a younger sister," he answered with a fond smile.

"Are you close?"

He laughed. "We are now. We hated each other when we were kids. Sibling rivalry, you know."

"No, I don't know," Callie said wistfully. She brushed back a lock of hair. "Being an only child can be very lonely, especially when—"

She clamped her mouth closed when she realized that she'd been about to say, *Especially when most parents don't want their children associating with the town floozy's daughter.* All the old hurts began to surface.

Not wanting to take another journey into the past, she challenged, "Race you to the top of the knoll!"

She took off running before Ian could answer. He broke into a lope that soon brought him up beside her, confirming just what he suspected; her tense posture and the guarded look in her eyes told him that she was running from her past. Instead of stopping, Callie veered off into the orchard when they reached the top of the knoll.

The path between the line of trees was too narrow for Ian to remain at her side, so he dropped behind her.

She broke out of the trees and came to a sudden halt at the edge of a small clearing. Ian was too close behind her to stop. When he realized he was probably going to land on top of her, he veered slightly, catching her waist, and twisted so that when he fell, she came down on top of him.

Callie was so stunned that she blinked in shock. "Ian, are you all right?" she asked worriedly.

"Wind . . . knocked . . . out . . . of . . . me," he gasped between ragged breaths. "You . . . should . . . carry . . . a . . . Stop . . . sign."

"Oh, Ian, I'm sorry," she said contritely. She tried to untangle herself from his limbs and let out a squeak of surprise when he rolled so that she was beneath him.

If Callie had been shocked when she found herself on top of him, she was rendered mute to find herself under him. She watched in mesmerized fascination as the pain in his eyes began to change. Callie knew lust when she saw it. But it wasn't just lust she saw reflected in Ian's face. It was something far more elemental and she reacted elementally. When he began to lower his head, she raised hers, meeting him halfway. As their lips mated, an intense wave of desire rolled through her. She moaned. Ian gave a groan of approval.

Ian hadn't meant to kiss Callie. When he found himself gazing into her wide blue eyes, he'd caught a glimpse of the hurt she kept locked inside and responded to her vulnerability. He told himself it was just going to be a short, soothing peck, but he lost all sense of time and place when Callie buried her hands in his hair and arched her supple body against his. She then kissed him so deeply, so wantonly, that within a heartbeat he was fully and achingly aroused.

He'd never experienced such a powerful attraction to a woman. He wasn't certain he wouldn't have taken her right then and there if a stranger's voice hadn't drawled, "I chase off teenagers all the time, but this is the first time I've had to chase off a couple old enough to have legal access to a bed."

Ian jerked his head up and flushed when he saw an elderly farmer leaning against a tree. He quickly glanced down at Callie, who had also flushed crimson. He then caught her head in his hand and cradled her face against his chest in a protective gesture.

He had to clear his throat before he could say, "Sorry. We didn't mean to trespass."

The farmer chuckled as he moved away from the tree. "Don't worry about it. I'd leave you alone, but I have a spraying crew coming this way, so you'd better take it home."

"You're right. Thanks," Ian said.

"Anytime."

Ian waited until the farmer was gone before he rose to his feet and helped Callie up, noting that she wouldn't look him in the eye. When she hurried back into the trees without a word, he followed slowly, considering what to say to her next. He knew she was mortified because he was equally mortified.

Ian raked both hands through his hair. He wasn't some randy teenager. What in the world had gotten into him? All he had to do was glance up and see Callie's retreating backside to know the answer. He cursed himself as again he got hard. Almost from the moment he'd laid eyes on her it had been as if he'd struck a match in a warehouse full of fireworks. He had a sinking feeling that all the fire fighters in the world weren't going to be able to put out these flames.

The best way to deal with Callie was to confront the issue head-on. When she reached the edge of the road, he lengthened his stride so he could catch up with her.

Callie's heart began to pound as she heard Ian closing the distance between them. It took every ounce of her courage to keep from breaking into a run. She couldn't believe that she'd just acted like some nymphomaniac on the loose. A blush of humiliation heated her cheeks—she could just *imagine* what Ian thought of her now. She refused to look at him after he caught up with her.

They walked for several minutes before Ian spoke. "I suppose I should apologize for what happened back there, but I'm not going to, because—"

His words hit Callie like a slap in the face, and she jerked her head toward him. "I wouldn't expect you to apologize," she interrupted coldly. "We both know that a tart from the wrong side of the tracks is fair game. What better way to get your kicks than to tumble her in the bushes?"

Enraged, he came to a stop, grabbed her arm and jerked her to his chest. "You know, Callie, sometimes I think that what you need is an old-fashioned paddling. I swear I'm going to give you one if I ever hear you demean yourself again."

"You and what army?" she challenged with a defiant lift of her chin.

Instead of answering, Ian strode away from her, sorely tempted to carry out his threat. The more he mulled over what she'd said, the angrier he got.

By the time he reached the motel, he recognized that he needed time to calm down. But the need to get this off his chest was stronger. He leaned against her door and waited for her.

His temper didn't improve when she approached him and said, "Move it or lose it, Sherlock."

He moved away from the door enough to allow her to unlock it. She tried to slip inside and slam it closed but he pushed his way in after her.

"This is my room. Get out!" she ordered as she faced him, her eyes blazing and her hands on her hips.

"I'll leave after you've explained your crack back there," he retorted as he slammed the door behind him.

"My crack!" she exclaimed in a low voice. "What about your crack?"

"That wasn't a crack. It was a statement of fact. Let me finish what I started to say. . . ."

Callie's mind halted at *It was a statement of fact*. She stalked over to him and jabbed her index finger against his chest. "You, Mr. Sherlock, are a first-class son of a—"

Ian placed his hand over her mouth. "Don't say something you're going to regret, Callie." When she glared at him, he removed his hand and continued, "As I was saying before I was so rudely interrupted, I meant what I said back there. I wasn't sorry for what happened, because I have never wanted a woman the way I want you. As furious as I am with you, I still want to haul you over to the bed, tear off your clothes, and make mad, passionate love with you. And you know it wouldn't be just a tumble, Callie, because you want me as much as I want you. You also know that what's happening between us is something special."

"Don't talk like that," she stated roughly.

"Why not? It's the truth."

Callie wanted to scream in frustration, because she knew he was right. She also knew she had to somehow rationalize this crazy hunger they had for each other for herself as much as for him.

"Look, Ian," she responded pleadingly. "What is going on between us is not something special. It's happening because we're on the run. Knowing that our freedom could be taken away from us at any moment has made us more volatile. When this is all over and our lives are back to normal, our emotions will subside. Then we'll wonder what we ever saw in each other."

Ian released a curt laugh. "Lady, if you believe that, I have some swampland you might be interested in." He opened the door. "When you get ready to conduct your 'discreet questioning,' let me know. I don't want you wandering around this rat hole without protection."

"Go to hell," Callie mumbled. But he was already gone.

She rubbed at her jaw as she walked to the door and locked it. Now her toothache was throbbing constantly. When she got her hands on Quincy, she'd strangle him with her bare hands!

"QUINCY, I THINK we should just go to the police and take our chances," Lincoln Galloway stated morosely. "It's bad enough that we got Ian into trouble. Now we've involved your niece. How many more innocent people are we going to bring down with us?"

Quincy grimaced. "We're not going to bring anyone down but the crooks, Lincoln." He held his index finger and thumb an inch apart. "We're this close to hanging them."

"We *were* that close, but lost our edge when the police raided the salvage yard." He sighed wearily. "I should have gone to Ian in the first place and told him what was going on. My God, I've worked for him for twelve years and he trusts me!"

"They were threatening your family, Lincoln. Loyalty begins at home," Quincy said, trying to assuage him. How was he going to soothe his own guilt over his treatment of Callie? He shouldn't have called the police, but he'd been trying to protect her. He'd find a way to get her out of this mess, he promised himself.

"That doesn't excuse what I've done," Lincoln responded with a heavy sigh. "It also doesn't explain why those men told the police that Ian was in charge of the operation when they'd already set me up to take the fall. Why did they do that, Quincy? Why did they frame Ian when they already had me framed? And why haven't the police come looking for either of us when we'd been managing the salvage yard? It doesn't make sense, Quincy. I don't like things that don't make sense."

"They framed Ian because we have the ledgers and they couldn't take the chance of them falling into the hands of the police. I don't know why the police haven't come looking for us. I'll lay odds that they've arranged that, too," Quincy replied.

"Look, Lincoln," he continued persuasively, "we've got the ledgers. The big boss knows that the information in them will cripple his operation. I can guarantee that he's sweating right now, and we're going to sit back and let him sweat. The longer we wait, the better chance we have of drawing him out. As soon as we know who he is, we can take him down."

Lincoln shook his head. "We're going to need more than his identity, and you know it. We have to be able to connect him directly to the thefts. We have to *prove* his involvement, and I don't know how we can do that."

Quincy grinned. "That's why I'm running this hustle. I know how to set him up, Lincoln. I'm going to make sure he's caught red-handed. Trust me."

Lincoln eyed him for a long moment, then agreed, "I guess at this point in time I don't have much choice. So why does my stomach feel as if it's on fire?"

"It's the thrill of the hustle," Quincy explained, his grin widening. "Take an antacid and call me in the morning."

"You're crazy," Lincoln muttered.

"I've been accused of worse in my life," Quincy said with a laugh.

"THE DOOR'S OPEN," Ian called out after he heard Callie's knock. He was kneeling on the floor, retrieving his shoe, which he'd accidentally kicked beneath the bed.

"Watch for mousetraps," Callie warned as she stepped into the room.

Ian pivoted his head toward her and froze when his eyes landed on a pair of sheer-stockinged feet encased in three-inch high-heeled sandals. He gulped as he let his gaze travel upward until he reached the hemline of a denim miniskirt. In skintight jeans, Callie's legs were gorgeous. In the flesh they were breathtaking, and Ian got hard instantly.

Down, boy! he told himself as he sat back on his heels and let his eyes wander all the way up. She was wearing a long-sleeved chambray shirt that provocatively displayed her admirable cleavage. On most women the outfit would have looked cheap; on Callie, it looked classy. Still, Ian was irritated with her because he knew she was wearing it for effect, not style.

"Mousetraps?" he repeated, planning to keep his opinion about her attire to himself.

"That's the proprietor's concession to pest control in places like these," Callie explained. She noticed Ian's bold surveillance of her body and shivered. "You'll find mousetraps under the bed most of the time. Look before you reach."

"Thanks for the warning." He returned to his search for his shoe. When he located it, he sat on the bed to pull it on. "What's the plan for this evening?"

"Well, I want to question some of our neighbors. If that turns up nothing, then we'll visit one of the pool parlors in the area. With any luck, we'll find Uncle Quincy."

"That makes sense. What if we don't find someone who's seen him? Do we just keep traveling down the road, or do we regroup?"

"We'll keep traveling down the road. If we aren't able to get a lead on him within a week then we'll regroup. But I hope we don't have to do that because I'm not sure where else to look for him. Uncle Quincy is normally a creature of habit. Right now he isn't behaving normally."

"Thanks. That was just what I wanted to hear," Ian stated ruefully.

"Would you rather I lied to you?" Callie asked.

"No." He went over to the battered dresser and picked up his wallet, stuffing it into his back pocket. "I prefer the truth, even if I don't like it. Let's get this show on the road."

Callie gnawed on her lower lip, torn about letting him accompany her because she just *knew* what his reaction was going to be to her "discreet" questioning. "While I'm checking with the neighbors, stay out of sight. Better yet, why don't you wait here? I'll be back before you know it."

Ian gave a firm shake of his head. "I saw one of our neighbors, Callie. There is no way I'm going to let you wander around this place by yourself. I'll hide in the shadows, but I'm going with you."

Callie was prepared to argue with him, but changed her mind after noting his determined expression. "All right," she agreed reluctantly. "You have to promise me, however, that you won't overreact. A lot of the people I'll be talking to are going to be extremely friendly."

"How friendly?" Ian asked suspiciously. His blood pressure rose significantly while he waited for her answer.

She widened her arms. "Take a look at me. How friendly would you be?" Ian's gaze raked over her again, and Callie shivered again.

"I'm not going to like this," he muttered when he redirected his eyes to her face. "In fact, I'm going to hate this."

"Well, you can hate it all you want—as long as you stay out of sight. If you come on like gangbusters, you're going to find yourself sitting in a jail cell, and the hunt for Uncle Quincy will be over."

"I'll keep that in mind if you'll make me a promise."

Callie eyed him warily. "That depends on what the promise is."

"I'll keep my distance if you promise to scream the instant you feel you might be in danger."

"You've got a deal, Sherlock," she said, praying that her relief wasn't evident in her voice. She didn't look forward to her "discreet" questioning any more than he did, but she didn't have a choice.

6

BY THE TIME CALLIE had finished her *discreet* questioning, Ian was fuming. If he'd had to witness one more man touching her, he was sure he'd have exploded. *Friendly* wasn't even close to what he'd seen. In fact, a few of her encounters had become so intimate that he'd had to turn his back on the scene to keep from interfering.

Ian's temper didn't improve as they headed for the car. Callie slid behind the steering wheel and began to hum the song "Some Enchanted Evening." He warned himself to keep his mouth shut, but couldn't resist saying, "Are you sure you don't want to go back to your room for a shower?"

Callie slowly turned her head toward him. "What's that supposed to mean?"

"Nothing," he stated tightly. "What did you find out?"

She started the car. "If Uncle Quincy's been here, no one knew it."

"So you were manhandled for nothing."

Callie turned off the car and shifted in her seat so she could face him. His tone of voice indicated he was looking for a fight. Might as well get it over with now. If she didn't, he'd stew all night. Eventually *something* would trigger his temper.

"I wasn't manhandled," she told him.

"Those men were all over you!" he exclaimed angrily.

"I wasn't manhandled," she repeated so reasonably that Ian got more furious.

"Then what in hell would you call it?"

"Friendly," she answered. "Manhandling means that someone treats you roughly. I was not treated roughly."

"They were all over you!" he insisted again.

"I was hugged a time or two. *No one* was all over me, Ian. If they had been, they would have found themselves flat on their backs. I'm very well trained in self-defense."

Ian glared at her. Damn, he wanted to throttle her! He closed his eyes and rubbed the bridge of his nose with his thumb and forefinger. All right, maybe those men hadn't been all over her. But they'd been too damn close to her for comfort.

"Did you enjoy it?" he asked, keeping his eyes closed so he wouldn't see her expression. If she had enjoyed it, he knew he would throttle her.

"What do you think?" she shot back, infuriated. "Dammit, Ian. I let a few men with bad breath and body odor give me a hug so I could get information on Uncle Quincy. Do you honestly believe I enjoyed subjecting myself to that?"

"No," Ian replied, opening his eyes and giving her a contrite look. "I'm overreacting. It's just that . . ."

"It's just that what?" Callie demanded when he didn't continue.

"I want you so badly. Watching those men touch you sent me over the edge." She parted her lips to respond, but Ian laid his fingers against them. "Don't say anything. Let's just get out of here."

Callie gripped the steering wheel in frustration, furious with him for thinking she could have enjoyed her earlier encounters. But there was so much vulnerability reflected in his face that she couldn't summon up the energy to yell at him. She'd known he'd react this way, so she should just forget about it. She didn't want him to think badly of her, however. She *had* to make him understand her actions.

"What you saw tonight was only an act," she said urgently. "I didn't like those men touching me. Sometimes we have to do things we don't like in order to achieve our goal. I can't help you clear your name without information. In order to get information, I'm going to have to do distasteful things. If I don't, you're going to go to prison. We both know you don't want that."

His own urgency surfacing, Ian reached for her. He threaded his fingers into her silken hair and hauled her face close to his as he said, "I think I'd rather go to prison than watch you do what you did tonight, Callie. Promise me you won't do it again."

Callie shook her head in despair. "I can't promise you that because I may have to do it again. Believe me, Ian—you wouldn't rather go to prison than watch a few repulsive men hug me. You're blowing the entire situation out of proportion. Why don't you take a deep breath and put everything in perspective?"

"I'm going to strangle Quincy when I get my hands on him," he muttered darkly, admitting she was right but averse to it.

A smile of understanding curved Callie's lips. "I'm afraid you'll have to stand in line for that honor. I put my bid in first."

Ian stroked his thumbs over her high cheekbones. "You're very beautiful when you smile. It makes you look as soft as you feel."

"I'm not soft," she denied, her smile turning wistful.

"Sure, you are." He trailed his hand down her cheek and stroked his thumb across her lower lip, sending electricity crackling through her. "You're just very good at hiding it. You don't have to hide from me, Callie. I'm not going to hurt you."

"Don't make promises you can't keep," she whispered, tears burning her eyes at the yearning his words evoked. All her life she'd craved to be loved and coddled and nurtured. That was *exactly* how Ian would treat the woman he fell in love with. Unfortunately she could never be that woman. "We'd better go."

"In a minute." He hooked a finger beneath her chin and tilted it upward as he lowered his head toward hers. "I have to take the feel of those men off you first."

"No!" Callie exclaimed in alarm, knowing that she couldn't let him kiss her right now.

Her objection came too late, and Ian took advantage of her parted lips to claim her. Her mind kept screaming that she had to fight him but her heart begged her to indulge in the moment. As soon as they found Quincy, Ian would be gone from her life. Would it be so wrong to go with her feelings until the inevitable happened? Probably—but she wanted Ian to do exactly what he'd said he was going to do: take the feel of those men off her.

She wound her arms around his neck, buried her fingers in his hair and burrowed against him. He responded with hunger, and she moaned when he settled one hand over a breast and the other high on her thigh. She trembled when he slid his hand beneath her skirt and began to stroke her inner thigh.

"Touch me," he rasped as he pulled away from her lips long enough to catch a breath.

"Where?" she mumbled.

"Anywhere you like."

He captured her lips again, and Callie's hands slid over him. His muscles seemed to leap beneath her touch as she explored his magnificent shoulders, chest and arms. He was so muscular, and she could feel his strength pulsing under her fingertips. She slipped her arms around him and traced his spine down to the waistband of his pants. When she drew her hands around his waist to his flat stomach, he jerked away from her.

Ian was breathing raggedly as he sat back in his seat. His body was on fire. The flames were fanned even higher when he risked a glance at Callie. Her lips were still parted and her eyes were glazed with passion. She'd come so close to settling her hands over his erection, and he knew that if she touched him there, he'd take her right in the car.

He'd never experienced such a powerful physical attraction to a woman, and it disturbed him. If her true self was Dr. Watson, he'd have no hesitation at all about what was happening between them. If she was really Doc Watson, he'd have to protect himself. He was not Lucy Coates. He couldn't become involved with a pool hustler who'd drift in and out of his life on a whim. This wild abandon he experienced every time he touched her could only lead to involvement. He had to figure which identity was the real Callie.

"If you don't get us out of this parking lot in five seconds, I refuse to be held accountable for my actions," he said.

His words broke through Callie's erotic daze. She quickly reached for the ignition, though every part of her body was screaming that she should let him carry out his threat. She'd never felt anything like this, and it frightened her.

Somehow she managed to get the car on the road. She couldn't become involved with Ian—she'd only be asking for trouble, and she already had enough trouble in her life.

Ian spoke when she braked for a light. "Are you finally ready to admit that what's occurring between us is more than just a side effect of being on the run?"

Callie nodded, then shook her head—unable to decide whether she was agreeing or disagreeing with his statement.

"So, what are we going to do about it?" he challenged.

"Do about it?" she whispered hoarsely.

Ian smiled reassuringly as he met her stare. He resisted the urge to reach out and brush the hair off her cheek; it was still too dangerous to touch her. Yet it was only a matter of time before they ended up in bed.

"Don't worry, Callie," he said. "I'm not going to pounce. When we make love, it will be a mutual decision."

She jumped when a horn blared behind her, telling her that the light had changed. She sent a prayer of thanks heavenward for the timely interruption. She needed a moment to pull herself together, because he hadn't said *if* we make love; he'd said *when,* and she knew he was right. It was going to happen no matter how hard she fought against it. If she'd been frightened before, she was now scared out of her wits; getting involved with a man like Ian could only lead to heartbreak.

"We can't get involved," she declared, grimacing at the quaver in her voice. She needed to sound firm, not like a trembling schoolgirl.

"I think we're already involved," he countered.

Callie shook her head impatiently. "We've struck some sparks, but that's it."

"We've lit the fire, and you know it."

"What do you want from me?" she railed as she risked a glance toward him.

"A chance."

"That's impossible," she muttered, returning her attention to the road.

"Why is it impossible?"

"Dammit, Ian," she groused as she pulled the car into a parking space in front of a run-down pool parlor. She threw the gearshift into Park, turned off the ignition and glared at him. "You're worse than a two-year-old kid with all your questions. Take my word for it, okay?"

"No. I want some answers. Why do you refuse to get involved with me?"

Callie glowered. He wasn't going to drop the subject, so she might as well tell him the truth and get it over with so he'd leave her alone. "We can't get involved, because when we find Uncle Quincy, I'll be going back to prison."

Before he could respond, she leaped out of the car and ran toward the pool parlor. Thankfully she made it through the door before Ian caught up with her—because she knew he would want to drown her with more questions. Eventually she'd have to answer them. At least now she'd have some time to consider how truthful she was going to be with him.

ENRAGED, IAN FOLLOWED Callie into the pool parlor. How dare she drop a bombshell like that and run? When he got his hands on her, he'd shake her until he got some answers. His anger was replaced by panic when he walked through the door and discovered that Callie was nowhere in sight.

She was gone, and he knew it. She'd known all along where Quincy was hiding and had just been waiting for an opportunity to ditch him so she could join her uncle. They'd disappear, and he'd be left holding the bag. He'd end up in prison, and he'd never—

His frantic thoughts were interrupted when Callie came out of the ladies' room and winked at him. He marched toward her, ready to give her the lecture of her life. When he reached her, she slid her arms around his waist and murmured throatily, "I see you finally found a parking spot, honey."

"Don't you *honey* me," he growled quietly as he settled his hands on her shoulders and gave her a fierce look. "I want some answers, and I want them now."

She smiled up at him and batted her lashes flirtatiously while muttering, "This is not the time or the place, Ian. When we get back to the motel, I'll answer all your questions. For now, you're going to smile and look bedazzled by me. You're a successful businessman out slumming, and you're going to let every man in this room know what your intentions are toward me."

"And what are my intentions supposed to be?" he drawled as he considered dragging her back to the car. He didn't want to wait for her answers, but the rebellious glow in her eyes told him that she'd talk when she was ready, and not one moment sooner.

He cursed when she slid one hand provocatively over his chest while dipping the other into his back pocket, resurrecting his desire. Her touch created a tumultuous combination of passion and fury. He'd never felt such conflict within himself. Flexing his fingers against her blouse, he fought the urge to haul her into his arms. He didn't know if he'd kiss her or squeeze the breath out of her.

"Use your imagination," she purred. "I've just added fifty dollars to your debt. It's in your back pocket. Follow my cue, and don't blow it, Ian."

"You're enjoying this, aren't you?" he accused as he noticed the excited gleam in her eyes.

"I always enjoy a good hustle. Pay the bartender for a table and get us a beer."

She walked away from him, her hips moving in an exaggerated sway that deserved a drumroll. She headed for a back table. Silence followed her in her wake as every game she passed came to a halt. Ian grabbed two mugs of beer and trailed after her. He didn't like her being ogled by a roomful of men. He didn't like it at all.

When he caught up with her, she gave him a brilliant smile. Ian forced himself to return it as he remarked, "That was quite a show."

"Glad you thought so. That means I did it right." She bent over the table to rack the balls. Ian turned a curse into a cough as her miniskirt hiked up a dangerous two inches.

"Having fun?" he taunted when she stood upright.

"Not yet, but the night's still young." She walked over to the nearby rack of cues and grabbed the first two. She tossed one to Ian. "Smile, Sherlock. Everyone is watching."

He bared his teeth at her. "I don't need to smile. They're not staring at my bottom."

She leaned sideways so she could survey his backside. "I don't know why. Your buns are darn cute."

"Make the break," he grumbled.

"Your wish is my command."

"Don't make promises you're not ready to keep."

Something flared in her eyes. Before Ian could determine what the emotion was, she said, "I won't." Then she leaned over the table and made the break.

For the next ten minutes, they didn't speak. Ian watched her play the game in amazement. He'd known she was good—she was a pool hustler, after all. But he'd never seen anyone in such command of the table. She shot ball after ball, unerringly making shots that were seemingly impossible. When she dropped the last ball into the pocket, she looked up at him and grinned.

"Well, Sherlock, what do you think?"

"That's the best game of nine ball I've ever seen. You must be fantastic at straight pool." He was enchanted to see a faint blush flare into her cheeks at the compliment, because he had the feeling that Doc Watson never blushed. Did that mean Dr. Watson rested closer to the surface than she let on?

"I'm not that good a player," she demurred. "I've never even come close to beating Uncle Quincy."

Ian mulled over her comment and another piece of the puzzle dropped into place. He'd been right. She dressed as she did because she doubted her skill as a pool player. Until she could beat her uncle, that myth would be perpetuated. She wasn't even aware of the competition she felt with Quincy. He also suspected that she wouldn't acknowledge it if he pointed it out to her.

"You're right," he said. "You're not good. You're fabulous!"

She laughed softly. "You're good for my ego."

Ian could only nod. She smiled at him, appearing so soft and approachable that he wanted to sweep her up into his arms and carry her out of there. He turned his attention to the table, telling himself that she might bring out the caveman in him, but he didn't have to act like one. The first order of business was finding Quincy. Then he could devote all his time to the thief's niece.

"I get to break this time," he reminded, "although I have a feeling it won't help me. I'm not a very good pool player. You'll be in control of the table before I know it."

"I could give you some pointers," she suggested.

"I'll take you up on the offer as soon as we find Quincy. In the meantime, how about letting me in on your plan? I assume we're here to do more than play pool."

For a moment, she'd been so lost in his admiring gaze that she'd forgotten about their search for Quincy. His reminder jolted her back to reality. When they caught up with Quincy, she'd never see Ian again, and she needed to keep that uppermost in her mind. If she didn't, she might do something stupid, like fall head over heels for the man.

"I don't know anyone here, so I'm trying to draw out the top stick," she informed him. "If Uncle Quincy's been within twenty-five miles of here, he'll know it."

"So why didn't you ask the bartender who the top stick is?" Ian asked as he readied himself for the break. "Why the charade?"

"It's called subtlety, Sherlock. We don't want to alert Uncle Quincy we're hot on his trail. Direct questions will arouse suspicion. If I manipulate the information out of the stick, he won't think anything about it."

Ian made the break and stood upright. He braced the cue between his feet and eyed her distrustfully. "Just how do you plan on manipulating the information out of him?"

"You'll see," she replied mysteriously.

"That's what I'm afraid of," he muttered grimly. He turned back to the table and studied the layout of the balls. He'd made a lousy break and had the feeling that he wouldn't even make the first shot. But then again, he hadn't thought he could make the shot yesterday when he'd made the bet with Callie, and yet he'd done it.

Yesterday? He was startled by the thought, because so much had happened since he'd first laid eyes on Callie that he found it impossible to believe only a day had passed. He noted that she was intently studying the balls on the table. He couldn't help but smile at her concentration.

Sensing his regard, she glanced toward him with a puzzled frown. "What are you grinning at, Sherlock?"

His smile widened. "You look so darn cute when you're concentrating. You get these little pucker lines between your eyebrows, and your nose crinkles."

"Pucker lines and crinkles?" Callie repeated, shaking her head in mock disgust. "I hope you don't use that line on all the girls, Sherlock. If you do, you're going to be one heck of a lonely man."

Ian laughed and looped his arm around her waist, drawing her to him. He brushed his nose against hers as he whispered, "You'll take pity on me, won't you?"

"Take pity on you?" she questioned. He pulled her even closer, making her aware of every hard line of his body down to his knees. It was enough to send any red-blooded woman into a tailspin, and Callie knew she was as red-blooded as they came. "Why should I take pity on you?"

"Because a man shouldn't be lonely at my age," he replied as he dropped a quick, hard kiss to her lips. "How am I doing?"

She peered at him in confusion. "How are you doing?"

"You told me to use my imagination so everyone would be clear about my intentions toward you."

Callie grappled with his answer. He was only acting. So why did she feel so damn irritated about it? "You're doing great, Sherlock. Keep up the good work."

"Oh, I intend to," he said, giving her bottom a fond pat.

Callie had the feeling that he was issuing her a warning. Once again, her self-protective instincts surfaced, and she eased out of his embrace. "Don't you think it's time you made a shot?"

Ian sensed her withdrawal, but he wasn't irritated by the walls she was erecting. He knew he was capable of breaching them.

You're on an ego trip! Ian shrugged off his nagging inner voice and made his shot. When it dropped into the pocket, he was ecstatic.

"Good shot, Sherlock!" Callie congratulated with enthusiasm.

With a smug grin, he readied himself for the next shot. His concentration was broken when Callie perched her elbows on the end of the table and ran her hand down the open neck of her shirt.

When he scowled at her, she smiled sweetly and said, "It's hot in here, isn't it?"

Ian admitted it was hot, but the environment didn't have a blessed thing to do with it. Callie was displaying enough cleavage to raise any man's temperature a good ten degrees. No, make that twenty and climbing. "You're trying to hustle me," he charged.

She widened her eyes innocently. "What a terrible thing to say. Why would I want to hustle you?"

"Habit," he surmised as his gaze wandered involuntarily down the front of her shirt. He was curious whether she had money stored in there tonight. The realization that she probably *did* raised his temperature another degree. "Button up, Callie. I demand a fair game out of you."

"Sorry, Sherlock, but I can't accommodate you. I can't convince the top stick that I'm Doc Watson if I don't live up to my reputation."

"Try telling him who you are. You'd be surprised how well the truth works."

She pursed her mouth. "Ahh, yes. The truth. It does have its merits. Believe me, Sherlock, a little sleight of hand works better in situations like these."

"I wouldn't be objecting to a little sleight of hand," he stated sullenly. "It's the eyeful of your many charms that has me on edge. Button up."

She gave him an insouciant smile and buttoned a button. She still had more bosom showing than Ian approved of. He decided to let it go. After all, she was most likely right. The stick would expect a certain amount of exposure from Doc Watson. Ian didn't like it but was going to have to live with it.

He managed to ignore her antics long enough to sink two more balls. That was it. Soon he had to turn the table over to her.

"What was that, Sherlock?" she asked with an innocent bat of her lashes when she heard him grumbling.

"I said that you're going to pay for that," he muttered. "I am not a graceful loser. Particularly when I'm being cheated."

Her smile didn't waver, but Ian would have sworn that he saw a flash of hurt in her eyes. He knew he was right when she said, "There is no way you can be a loser at this table, Ian. We aren't playing a game of pool. We're playing for your life."

"Callie—" He cursed himself for hurting her feelings. She was trying to help him, so why was he picking on her? Because he still couldn't figure out who she really was, and it was driving him crazy.

"Forget it, Sherlock," she interrupted coolly. "You're only acting in character, so stop taking it personally. We're supposed to be working as a team. If you can't handle the pressure, I'll take you back to the motel and do this on my own."

The moment the words were out of her mouth, Callie knew she'd gone too far. The fury in Ian's eyes confirmed it. He might be easygoing, but still he had an ego, and she'd just stomped on it.

"Ian, I'm sorry. That was uncalled for," she blurted out, hoping to pacify him before his temper erupted. "You hurt my feelings, and I guess I was getting my revenge."

"I am not a babe in the woods," he declared irritably.

"Of course, you're not," Callie agreed. She was relieved that he'd been so easily pacified. However, as far as she was concerned, Ian was too nice for his own good—everyone knew that nice guys finished last.

"I'm thirty-five years old," he told her. "I own my own business, and it's a *big* business. I didn't become successful by accident. I worked hard at it, Callie. Damned hard. And I don't appreciate being treated like some incompetent fool."

"I'm sorry," Callie murmured.

"I'm the one who's sorry." Ian sighed heavily. "You're trying to help me, and I shouldn't be complaining about your methods. It's just that . . ."

"It's just that what?" Callie prompted when his voice trailed off.

He shook his head and gave her a rueful smile. "It's not important. Make your shot."

She guessed what he'd started to say—that he expected her to play by his rules, not the ones according to Watson.

She turned away from him, pretending to concentrate on her shot. For a moment, she couldn't see a thing through the blur of tears. It wasn't the first time Callie had felt ashamed of the life she led; nevertheless, it was the first time she had felt disappointed in herself.

Six games later, Ian was ready to tear out his hair in frustration. He'd apologized for his earlier faux pas. No matter how many times he replayed the conversation, he couldn't figure out what he'd said to make her so upset.

And he recognized she was upset. There was a look of frenzy in her eyes, and her smile was too bright. Her banter was forced, and her hard edge was honed to razor sharpness. To make matters worse, she was continually touching him for the benefit of their audience. Ian's body had long ago passed the stage of arousal.

Now he was existing in erotic hell. Once this game was over, they were getting out of there. But as she made another shot, a man started for their table.

"I think the top stick's finally taken the bait," he murmured.

Callie glanced up at him, but didn't turn her head. "Tall, pencil slim, thinning black hair and ugly enough to stop a clock?"

"You knew who he was all along?"

Callie shook her head. "I figured it out a couple of games ago. He was the only man in the place not gawking at us. His disinterest was too obvious. Play it cool, Sherlock."

"In other words, keep my mouth shut."

She sank her next ball. "You said it, not me."

"Well, I can read your mind."

"Good heavens, I hope not." She dropped her cue to the floor and leaned on it. "My mind is muddled enough. I don't need someone else in there muddying up the waters. Kiss me, Sherlock. We need to convince the man that I'm here out of lust, not sport."

Ian eagerly complied with her order because it had been uppermost in his mind for the past hour. He groaned softly when she pulled away, trailing her hand down his chest.

"Tease," he accused mildly, only to have her flash him a sassy grin.

"Hello," the man greeted as he came near.

"Hi," Callie replied, turning toward him with a welcoming smile. "I'm Callie." She extended her hand.

"Slim," he provided as he accepted it.

"Slim!" she exclaimed, casting a look of incredulity toward Ian. "Sherlock, this is *Slim*."

The man visibly preened. "You've heard of me?"

"Heard of you?" Callie repeated in awe. "Why, my uncle raved about you. He said you were the best pool player he'd seen in years."

"And your uncle is?" he inquired curiously.

"Quincy," Callie answered.

"You're related to Quincy?" Slim questioned in surprise.

"She's Doc Watson," Ian announced.

"*You*'re Doc Watson?" the man repeated in disbelief. Ian didn't miss the fact that his beady eyes immediately dropped to the neckline of Callie's blouse. He wanted to punch Slim in the nose, but he stuffed his hands into his pockets instead.

"I'm Doc," Callie acknowledged.

"Looking for a game?" he asked as he dragged his leer upward.

"No, she's not," Ian stated abruptly, ignoring Callie's chastising look. "We're just having some fun."

Slim leaned on his cue. "We could make it lucrative."

Callie pursed her lips as if considering his words. "I'm sorry, Slim," she finally said, casting a calf-eyed glance toward Ian, "but my friend and I have plans."

"Big plans," Ian added, placing an arm around her waist and pulling her to his side in a proprietary gesture.

Slim's smile was bordering on lecherous as his gaze once again wandered down to Callie's décolletage. Ian could read every lustful thought running through the man's mind. Punching him in the nose almost seemed too trivial a reaction. He also wanted to blacken both of his eyes.

"Maybe you can talk her into a game after we find Quincy," Ian continued, ignoring Callie's warning glare. He didn't care if she had told him to keep his mouth shut. He wasn't going to stand there and watch the lecher mentally undress her. He was going to get the information they needed and haul her out of here. "You haven't seen him, have you? He said we'd eventually find him if we made the rounds when we arrived. So far, we haven't had any luck."

Slim shook his head. "I haven't seen him. I can guarantee he isn't at any of the other parlors in the area. I would have heard."

"Well, that doesn't surprise me," Callie replied. "He probably ran across a good game and forgot all about us." She smiled at Ian, though she was seething. How dare he take command of the situation? The moment they were out of there, she was going to set him straight. She was in charge, and he'd better not forget it! "Too bad, Sherlock. I guess you won't get to meet Quincy this time around."

"Well, there's always next time," Ian said, returning her smile. Then he lowered his voice suggestively. "Let's get out of here. I have an early appointment at the office tomorrow. If I'm going to get there on time, I'm going to have to leave before dawn."

"That early?" Callie murmured in feigned disappointment. "You're always in such a rush, Sherlock. If I didn't know better, I'd think you were only interested in my body."

"Now, sweetheart, you know that's not true," Ian told her. "I'm just a busy man."

"Well, next time I expect an entire weekend with you." Callie lifted her cue and took Ian's from his hand.

Slim's eyes bulged as he watched her swaying bottom when she walked to the rack to replace them. "Some men have all the luck," he mumbled, his envy obvious. "Nice to meet you, Doc," he stated when Callie returned. "After your friend is gone, come back for a game."

"I'd love to, Slim. But I have to leave town in the morning. I'll be back soon. Next time I'll take you up on the offer."

"I look forward to it." He accepted Callie's outstretched hand. Ian noted that his eyes never left her bustline.

When Slim finally walked away, Ian grabbed Callie's elbow and began rushing her toward the door, saying, "We're getting out of here."

Callie didn't speak until they were on the sidewalk. There, she jerked her arm out of his hold and thrust her hands on her hips, glowering at him. "Just what were you trying to prove in there? You almost blew everything by telling him we were looking for Uncle Quincy."

"The man was undressing you with his eyes!" Ian snapped.

"That's what he was supposed to be doing!" Callie snapped back. "Dammit, Ian, we have to ask our questions with finesse. If we don't, Uncle Quincy will find out that we're looking for him. Then we'll never find him! From now on, keep your mouth shut! Let *me* run with the ball."

She stalked toward the car. She was trying to help the man, and he seemed determined to sabotage her. If she had any sense, she'd turn him over to the cops and look for Quincy on her own. At least in jail, Ian wouldn't be screwing things up and she might have a decent chance of saving his hide.

With a curse, she jerked open the door. Ian reached over her shoulder and slammed it shut, and she let out a startled yelp. He gripped her shoulders and spun her around to face him. Callie gulped. He was livid, and she cringed. Just the same, she assumed a belligerent stance against the door.

"Got a problem, Sherlock?"

"You're damn right I've got a problem," he retorted. He placed a hand on either side of her head, trapping her against the car. "I want your help, Callie, but not at the price of my moral standards."

Her chin rose. "Are you calling me immoral?"

"No. I'm calling you misguided." His eyes dropped to the front of her blouse. He wanted to groan when he saw that her defiant posture had opened the neckline even farther. He wanted to bury his lips between her alabaster breasts, and then he wanted to— He brought his imagination to an abrupt halt. Otherwise he was no better than the lecherous Slim. It wasn't just her body he was interested in. It was the whole wonderful, maddening package.

"It's not your fault," he said, forcing his gaze back to hers. "You haven't exactly had the best role models in your life. But you know that what you're doing is wrong. Start using your brain instead of your body, Callie. You'll feel better about yourself."

"I feel just fine about myself, Sherlock. You're the one who has the problem," she stated defensively.

His anger suddenly dissipated. "You're lying to yourself, Callie, and you know it. So why do you insist on doing it?"

"Why shouldn't I do it, Sherlock? After all, if you have the name, you might as well play the game."

"What does that mean?"

She shrugged impatiently. "Nothing. Let's go back to the motel."

"Fine. There you can explain the bombshell you dropped earlier."

Callie's stomach lurched at his words. If Ian felt as if his moral standards had been compromised before, how in the world was he going to react when she explained her more recent past? Not well. And she knew it. Maybe she could avoid his question. Maybe she should lie. Maybe—

No. She was going to tell him the truth. Once he knew it, he wouldn't be complaining about her attire, and he'd let her do what she had to do to help him. The thought should have been reassuring, but all it did was hurt.

"Let's go, Sherlock," she stated wearily as she placed a hand against his chest and pushed.

Ian reluctantly stepped away from her. He regarded her with concern. For once, she wasn't hiding behind a mask; her pain was clearly visible.

He raised a hand to touch her, to comfort her, but she turned her back on him and climbed inside the car. Ian felt an apprehensive shiver crawl up his spine. Did he really want to know the truth about her?

7

CALLIE NEVER DRANK more than a couple of beers while playing pool or an occasional glass of wine with dinner. After climbing out of the car, she eyed the state liquor store across from the motel. A belt of something strong was appealing. As she considered buying a bottle, the image of her mother flashed through her mind. She turned and walked toward her room.

Ian had been silent during the drive, and she observed him while he walked in step with her. His posture was stiff—which only increased her tension. She liked Ian and didn't want to be diminished in his eyes, even if it would be the best thing for both of them. The attraction between them was too strong. Any involvement with him would only lead her to hurt and humiliation. After all, Doc Watson wasn't the type of woman you took home to meet Mom and Dad.

"Have a seat, Sherlock," she said, gesturing toward the foot of her bed when they entered her room. She sat on top of a low dresser with a cracked mirror. "So, what do you want to know?"

"You said that when we found Quincy, you'd be going back to prison. Is that true?"

Callie nodded. "I'm an ex-con. When I became involved with you, a wanted man, I broke my parole.

Since I have a year left on my sentence, I'll be completing it in jail."

He frowned at her. "That's ridiculous, Callie. When we find Quincy, we'll prove I'm innocent, which means you'll have been involved with an innocent man. They can't send you to prison for that. It wouldn't be fair."

"We aren't talking about fair, Sherlock. We're talking about the law." She kicked off her shoes and rubbed one foot on top of the other, then reversed the procedure. "I knowingly became involved with a wanted man. Instead of turning you over to the police like a good citizen should, I helped you elude them. If we find Uncle Quincy and prove your innocence, I might be able to convince my parole officer to go to bat for me and plead extenuating circumstances, but it will be up to the judge to decide my fate. I'm afraid the judges in Queen's County aren't too fond of women like me. We corrupt their children."

Ian stared at her implacable face. "Why were you in prison?"

She didn't even bat an eye as she said, "I was convicted of solicitation, robbery and assault and battery."

"I don't believe it," Ian muttered.

"Oh, believe it, Sherlock," Callie countered dryly. "I've got the mug shots to prove my incarceration."

"Oh, I believe you were in prison, Callie. But you'd never do any of those things," he stated with conviction.

"The judge and the district attorney would disagree with you."

"The judge and the district attorney don't know you."

He came toward her. Callie knew that she should be hopping off the dresser before he could trap her. She was too fascinated by his response, however, to move. All she had to do was look in his eyes to know that he honestly believed she was innocent. The fact that he did was mind-blowing.

"Tell me what happened, Callie," he urged when he stood in front of her. "Maybe I can help you."

She gave him a wry smile. "You can't help me, Sherlock. Out of curiosity, why are you so sure I'm innocent?"

He caught her chin in his hand and traced her jawline with his thumb. "Because I know you. Tell me what happened."

Callie couldn't decide which she found more confusing to her senses—his gentle touch or the warm encouragement in his eyes. Before she even knew what she was doing, she heard herself whisper, "What happened? I guess you could say I fell in love."

Ian felt as if he'd just been punched in the stomach at her words, and he couldn't understand why. But that wasn't entirely true, he suddenly realized. His attraction to her was so strong he couldn't stand the thought of another man touching her.

"Who was he?" he asked, his voice brusque.

"One of my college professors," Callie replied.

"How could falling in love with a college professor land you in prison?" he questioned in confusion.

"He got himself into a financial jam, and I began to hustle pool again to bail him out," Callie confessed with an embarrassed shrug.

"You began to hustle pool *again?*"

She nodded and raked both hands through her hair. "Ian, I need to move around if I'm going to tell you this story."

He was reluctant to pull away, but he could feel her agitation and understood her need to pace. He dropped his hand from her chin and walked back to the bed.

Callie jumped off the dresser and prowled about the room, trying to organize her thoughts. Finally she drew in a deep breath for the courage to begin.

"You were right. Getting my doctorate was a challenge, but it wasn't as much a challenge as an effort to legitimize myself. Do you know what I'm saying?"

"Sure," Ian answered. "You wanted people to be able to look up to you because you'd spent most of your life being looked down upon."

"Yeah," she agreed, chagrined by his ability to express her motives so simply. She wasn't sure she could have done it as well. "Well, back to my story. I didn't have the money to go to college, so I hustled pool to pay for my education. By the time I started on my doctorate, however, I realized I needed to stop hustling if I wanted people to respect me as an academic. I had excellent grades and was able to land a few grants. I became a research assistant for Steven to supplement my income."

She lifted the curtain at the window, ignoring the dust that billowed from it as she peered out into the darkness. "Steven was such an intense man. I'd never met anyone like him."

"And you fell in love with him," Ian added.

"It happened gradually," Callie murmured, dropping the curtain back into place and turning to look at him. "I decided to do my dissertation on the gypsy-moth infestation in our area. They had decimated thousands of acres of trees. I wanted to see what effects their loss had had on other plant life. Steven was enthused about the project and offered to share some of his research with me. We spent a lot of time together and . . . my admiration for him grew into love."

Ian didn't say anything when she lapsed into silence, because he was experiencing what felt suspiciously like the stirrings of jealousy. He told himself he was being ridiculous, but it didn't negate the feelings.

Callie's eyes had a faraway look when she continued, "I'd never had anyone treat me like Steven did. I adored him. And when I found out he'd made some bad investments in the stock market and was in financial straits, I offered to help him out."

"So you started hustling pool again," Ian prompted. When Callie nodded, he asked, "How did Steven feel about that?"

"He wouldn't have liked the truth, so I told him I had a part-time job."

"And the lie backfired on you."

"Boy, did it backfire on me!" She leaned against the wall and closed her eyes. "I was playing regularly at Kelly's. One night a group of half-drunk men came in. One of them was flashing a bankroll, just begging to be hustled. Mick told me he had a bad feeling about the guy and that I should leave him alone. I've never been good at taking advice, so I offered to play him a few games. He laughed at me, saying that everyone knew pool was a man's game and that women weren't any good at it. That only made me more determined to hustle him. He finally agreed to play me so he could teach me a lesson."

"Instead, he got taught a lesson," Ian guessed wryly.

"Yes. I wiped out his bankroll in an hour. He was angry when he stormed out of Kelly's, but I didn't realize just *how* angry. I'd embarrassed him in front of his friends. I quickly learned that he didn't handle embarrassment well."

She opened her eyes and gave Ian a grim smile. "When I left, he was waiting for me in the parking lot. I'd dealt with angry drunks before, so I was sure I could talk my way out of the situation. But it soon became apparent that he had been infuriated to the point of violence. I tried to get to my car, but he swung at me. I saw the blow coming, and I was able to deflect it. I retaliated by hitting him over the head with my cue case. Then I hightailed it out of there without even stopping to see how badly he was hurt."

"And how badly was he hurt?" Ian queried, only able to control his rising temper by clenching his hands into fists. Just the thought of someone trying to strike her was enough to send him into a rage.

"Badly enough to require stitches, but not so badly that he rushed to the hospital. It later became apparent that he and his buddies had followed me home."

She released a heavy sigh before continuing. "The next morning the police showed up at my door and told me that I was being arrested for solicitation, theft and assault and battery. I was so dumbfounded by the first two accusations that I agreed to let them search my house and my car. They found his money in my apartment, of course. They also found his wallet in my car."

"How did his wallet get in your car?" Ian asked in surprise.

"He had to have put it there. You see, he told the police that we had met at Kelly's and that I'd propositioned him while we played a few games of pool. He claimed that we'd made our assignation in the parking lot and I'd brought him to my apartment, at which time I hit him over the head, knocking him unconscious, and then stole his wallet. I admitted to hitting him, explaining not only that it had happened at Kelly's, but that it was also a case of self-defense. Unfortunately, since I'd deflected his blow, I didn't have any bruises to prove it."

"How in hell did he get the other charges to stick?" Ian questioned.

"His buddies testified that they'd heard me proposition him, and that they'd agreed to pick him up at my apartment. They said that when they arrived, they found him lying unconscious in the parking lot."

"Why didn't Mick come to your defense? He knew you'd hustled the guy and he was angry about it."

"Mick did step forward, but that would have only been opening up another can of worms," Callie told him. "Gambling is illegal in Pennsylvania, and playing pool for money is considered gambling. My attorney recommended that I not bring it up because the shuddered violently as the loud, metallic slam of prison doors reverberated in her mind.

If anyone had told her she could hate Quincy, she would have called them a liar. But at that moment, she hated him with the same ferocity with which she'd always loved him. Not only had he stolen away her precious freedom, but because of him, Ian had stormed into her life and made her want to start chasing rainbows again. She didn't think she'd ever be able to forgive her uncle for that. She'd learned the hard way that there was no pot of gold at the end of the rainbow for Calandra Elizabeth Watson.

She dabbed impatiently at her tears and went to bed. Maybe a good night's sleep would lift her spirits.

Once she was in bed, sleep eluded her. She kept hearing Ian saying, *You've convinced yourself that you're Doc Watson, but you know you're really Dr. Watson. I'm going to prove that to you.*

Callie lay staring up at the ceiling. It would be easy to fall in love with Ian, and she simply couldn't allow herself to do that. In the first stage of love, he might be able to tolerate the whispers and innuendos his family and friends would make about her. Inevitably his tolerance would fade. She'd had enough rejection in her life and wasn't about to set herself up for more.

As the hours crept by, Callie concluded that there was only one way she could discourage Ian and protect herself. Dr. Watson would have to disappear and Doc Watson would have to reappear—more flamboyantly than ever.

judge would probably just have added the charge of gambling to my crimes."

Ian's curse was low but succinct. "That's ridiculous! Everyone knows that money frequently changes hands in a pool hall."

"Everyone knows it, Ian. Normally they turn a blind eye to it. I couldn't afford to take that chance. I'd already admitted to hitting the man, and his cronies were the only witnesses to what had happened. Dragging Mick into it wasn't going to change anything. Plus, it was my fault I was in the mess I was in. The first rule Uncle Quincy taught me about hustling is that you never bankrupt your opponent. People don't mind losing a few bucks, but they do mind being wiped out. I broke that rule—and paid for it."

Ian mulled over her story. Finally he asked, "What happened with Steven?"

She dropped her gaze to the floor, but not before he noticed the flash of pain in her eyes. "Steven had an image to uphold at the college and couldn't afford to be involved with a convicted felon." She didn't bother to add that Steven had believed every charge against her and had turned away in disgust.

Ian resisted the urge to slam his fist into the wall. Besides, it was so thin that his arm would probably go through it. He was livid, and he couldn't determine whom he was more furious with—Quincy, for teaching her how to hustle in the first place; Steven, who'd used her and then deserted her; or the man whose wounded machismo had unfairly sent her to prison.

There was also a part of him that was furious with Callie. Why wasn't she putting her degree to use, instead of reverting to the life-style that had gotten her into trouble in the first place?

He eyed her thoughtfully. He recalled her telling him that Quincy couldn't give a two-week notice when quitting a job because the lure of the tables was too great to ignore. Was *that* why she was hustling rather than using her degree? Was she addicted to the thrill? he speculated, remembering the excited gleam in her eyes when she'd told him tonight that she always enjoyed a good hustle.

Before he could even begin to come up with some answers, Callie said, "I think we'd better call it a night. We need to get an early start in the morning."

"I'm not going to leave, Callie. We need to talk about this."

She shook her head. "There's nothing to talk about."

"Yes, there is," Ian countered resolutely. "Dammit, Callie, something is happening between us, and you're fighting against it because of your past. Start dealing with the present. With *us*."

"Stop talking that way!" she ordered impatiently.

"Why?" Ian demanded.

"Because we come from two different worlds," she answered. "If it hadn't been for Uncle Quincy, we'd never have met. Think about it, Ian. Am I the type of woman you'd want to take home to meet your family?"

He regarded her for a long moment. "That would depend."

"On what?"

"On if you're Doc Watson the pool hustler, or Dr. Watson the botanist. Which woman are you, Callie?"

"Doc Watson," she replied staunchly.

"I don't believe you." He walked over to her an tapped his finger against her temple. "Up here, you' convinced yourself that you're Doc Watson. But here—" he tapped his finger against her chest "—you Dr. Watson. I'm going to make you accept that."

"You're making threats again," she muttered ir bly.

"No," he insisted. "I'm making a promise."

"Just leave, Ian," she murmured, too weary to with him any longer.

Ian stared at her with indecision. Maybe he s do as she requested. Or should he stay and fight They'd already had too many confrontations and perhaps it was best they got some breathing

"All right, Callie," he agreed. "But this isn' With that, he turned and walked out. Callie s on the edge of her bed and buried her face in he

You are what you were born to be, and the so come to grips with it, the sooner it stops hu chanted silently. The pain didn't go away, only got worse. Tears rolled down her cheeks she crying? Why?

Because Ian represented that shimmering the horizon that she'd chased from childho the epitome of home and hearth and the far was the house with the white picket fence tion wagon filled with children and a tail- He was everything she'd yearned for for could remember—and would yearn for she died. He was everything she could r

WHEN CALLIE OPENED her door the next morning and handed Ian her suitcase, his jaw dropped and his eyes bulged. She had on a pair of stone-washed, hip-hugging denims that laced up the front and were so tight he couldn't see how she could breathe, let alone move. However, her pants were demure compared to her blouse—which not only had a plunging neckline, but ended just under her breasts, thus baring her midriff to a few inches below her navel. If it hadn't been for the long sleeves covering her arms, Ian could have used the scrap of fabric as a handkerchief.

"What in hell are you wearing?" he demanded.

Callie glanced down at herself before calmly replying, "Clothes."

"Those aren't clothes. They're . . . they're . . ."

"They're clothes, Ian."

He would have raked both hands through his hair, but they were holding the suitcases. "Dammit, Callie. Those pants are so tight they've probably cut off your circulation!"

She gave a careless shrug. "If you see my toes turning blue, let me know."

When she slid past him, Ian's jaw dropped even further as he watched her walk to the car in strapless spike-heeled sandals so high she'd probably break her neck if she fell off them. The back of her blouse was nothing more than two narrow strips that held her sleeves in place and the bustline closed. My word! The woman was half-naked, and he was so turned on he couldn't move!

She opened the trunk of Lucy's car. Ian sucked in a harsh breath as he watched her blouse ride up against her breasts. He kept his eyes averted from her when he joined her.

But after he dropped the suitcases into the trunk and closed the lid, he had to face her. His eyes drifted down to the apex of her thighs where the denim clung to her seductively. He had to clear his throat before he could speak. "Maybe you'd better let me drive, Callie. I'm not sure you can react fast enough in those pants if you're faced with an emergency."

"Whatever," she said with another careless shrug and handed him her keys.

Maybe he should let her drive, after all. At that moment, his own pants were so tight he feared he was in danger of injuring himself.

"Damn you, Quincy McKiernan," he muttered as he rounded the car. "Why didn't you raise her in a decent environment so she wouldn't be so insecure?" That was what this was all about. He'd told her last night that he was going to prove to her that she was really Dr. Watson, whereas this morning she seemed determined to prove him wrong.

"What was that, Ian?" Callie asked when he slid in beside her.

"I said it's darned hot for this early in May." He shifted in his seat, trying to find a comfortable position. Finally he gave up and fastened his seat belt. "Where are we headed?"

"Take a left and follow your nose," she directed as she fastened her own seat belt. "Since any top stick will know if Uncle Quincy is within a twenty-five mile radius, and since we know he isn't in this area, we might as well put in a good fifty miles today."

"Great." He backed out of the parking space. Fifty miles should give him enough time to cool down, provided that he could keep his eyes on the road—a most unlikely possibility.

Callie leaned her head against the window as they drove out of town. Ian was silent. What was he thinking?

"May I ask you a question?" he suddenly said.

"Sure," Callie answered.

"You said Quincy was your mother's brother. How come your name is Watson and not McKiernan?"

"They were half brother and sister. Uncle Quincy's father died when he was a boy, and my grandmother remarried."

"I see. Are your grandparents alive?"

"No. It's just Uncle Quincy and me. Are your grandparents alive?"

He nodded. "All four of them are alive and well."

"That's wonderful. What are they like?"

"All different. My mother's parents are sober and correct. My father's parents are hell-raisers."

"How do they raise hell?" Callie asked, intrigued.

"Any way they can. Just last month they had a wild party and nearly got arrested for disturbing the peace."

"How old are they?" Callie questioned with a delighted laugh.

"Grandpop's seventy-eight, and Nana's seventy-six. You wouldn't know it to meet them." He smiled at her. "He drives a Corvette and she drives a Porsche. They drag-race each other, and have more speeding tickets than most teenagers."

"I love it!" she exclaimed with another delighted laugh.

"I thought you would," he said seriously. "It was important to me that you did."

Callie blinked in surprise. "Why was it important to you?"

"Because I gave you the wrong impression last night. I'd be as pleased to take Doc Watson home to meet my family as I would Dr. Watson."

"Stop it, Ian," Callie whispered hoarsely as she turned her head and stared out the passenger window.

"I'm not going to stop it, Callie, because I know what you're doing. You put on that ridiculous outfit today because you wanted to discourage me. I don't discourage that easily."

Damn the man and his infallible insight! "Well, if you don't, then you're a fool. What your grandparents pull are high jinks. I have a criminal record. That isn't an escapade you can laugh off," she stated firmly. "That's a scandal, Ian. It's the kind of scandal that stays with you—the kind of scandal that makes people whisper about you and taints everyone around you."

"But you were innocent, Callie."

"The law says I'm guilty!" she railed at him. "When are you going to get it through your thick head that I am anathema to you? You might feel you can handle it now. I guarantee you won't feel that way once your libido's satisfied. My prison record is never going to disappear."

"People don't need to know any more about you than you're willing to tell them," he argued. "You have options, Callie. You have a Ph.D. in botany. For God's sake, stop hustling pool, settle down in a nice, quiet neighborhood and get yourself a respectable job."

"That's easy for you to say. I'm nearly thirty. What do I put down for past work experience on a job application? A little part-time landscaping and a lot of full-time basket weaving in prison? That'll go over well."

"Start your own business, then," Ian said. "Go into landscaping yourself. Open a flower shop. Be your own boss."

Callie rolled her eyes. "Good heavens, Ian, I can't even qualify for a credit card, so how am I supposed to get a small-business loan? And I don't know why we're having this conversation in the first place. I'm going back to prison within a matter of weeks."

He shot her a look of reproach. "You aren't going back to prison, Callie. I got you into this mess, and I'll get you out of it."

Callie gave a despairing shake of her head. "You're so damn naive. The facts jump up and bite you, and you refuse to accept them. But even if you do manage to keep me out of prison, it still won't change what I am. Let's drop the subject, okay? I'm bored with it."

When the car swerved out of control, Ian braked so hard she was thrown forward against her seat belt. Before she had a chance to recover, Ian yanked open her car door, unfastened her seat belt and dragged her out of the car.

"What are you doing?" she demanded angrily as he hauled her into the woods. The heel of her shoe caught on the brush. She started to fall, and Ian caught her around the waist and swung her up into his arms. "Put me down!" she yelled at him.

"When I'm ready," he muttered as he continued tramping into the woods. After they'd arrived at a small clearing, he dropped her to her feet. "Okay, you're down."

Callie glowered at him. "What do you think you're doing?"

He folded his arms over his chest and studied her for several seconds before he spoke. "You remind me of a stray cat I found in the woodpile when I was ten years old. He'd been in a fight and was beaten to a pulp. I wanted to take him to the vet, but no matter how much I coaxed, he wouldn't come near me. My dad said I had to gain his trust. Every morning I took him a plate of food, and then I'd sit there for hours trying to convince him that I wasn't going to hurt him. Nevertheless, that cat would rather suffer than let me help him. One day I went out to the woodpile and he was dead. I was furious at that cat for dying unnecessarily. My dad explained that he was just 'a dumb animal.' You're not a dumb animal, Callie, so stop hiding in the woodpile."

"Go to hell," Callie retorted and started to march past him. Ian grabbed her arm and spun her around to face him. She opened her mouth to shout at him. Before she could utter a word, his lips covered hers.

Fight! her mind screamed. She didn't have a chance—Ian caught her hips and pulled her against him. His arousal was her undoing. She arched against him, moving against him insistently.

"Easy, sweetheart. Easy," Ian rasped, easing out of their kiss. "I'm not going to make love to you in the bushes. Keep that up, and I'm going to have an embarrassing stain on the front of my trousers."

"Oh, my God, what am I doing?" Callie exclaimed in mortification. Ian caught the back of her head and cradled her against his chest.

"You're only doing what comes naturally." He rested his cheek against her hair. "Relax, Callie."

"You scare the hell out of me," she whispered. "I didn't even know you until a couple of days ago, so why do you make me feel like this?"

Ian swept his hand up her bare back. "Maybe it's kismet."

She raised her head and stared up at him in worried concern. "It can't work between us, Ian. You have to admit that."

He tenderly brushed her hair away from her cheek. "You may be right, Callie. We won't know that for certain unless we give it a chance. Why don't we just take it a day at a time?"

Still convinced that it could never work, Callie realized that Ian had to discover the truth for himself. The only way he could do that was for her to give him the chance he wanted.

"All right, Ian," she finally agreed with a resigned sigh. "We'll take it a day at a time."

8

CALLIE PROWLED AROUND her motel room, inflicted with the claustrophobia she'd developed in prison. She was lying to herself—again. Her restlessness had less to do with her confinement and more to do with Ian.

It had been five days since she'd told him she'd take everything a day at a time. The passion between them was as strong as ever. Yet he hadn't come near her. When she'd asked him what he was up to, he'd said, "I'm keeping my distance. We need some time to get to know each other."

He couldn't have chosen a better way to torment her. Callie threw herself down on the bed in frustration. She should be pleased that he was keeping his distance. She couldn't afford to become involved with him. As soon as they found Quincy, she'd be going back to prison—no matter what Ian said to the contrary. If by some miracle she did remain free, still there was no future for them. He was the all-American guy next door; she was...

Heaven help her! She didn't know who she was anymore. Rolling onto her stomach, she buried her face in her pillow to muffle her groans. She couldn't take much more of Ian's nice-guy routine. She was sure she was going to end up in a padded cell. They'd better find Quincy soon, or...!

She got up and resumed her pacing. Their search for him was a total bust. In six days, she and Ian had hit eleven pool parlors. In not one of them had she run across one of Quincy's close friends. That in and of itself was suspicious. Something must be happening on the circuit that she didn't know about. Tonight she'd ask some questions to find out where the action was.

Her thoughts were interrupted by a knock, followed by a muffled "It's Ian." He'd gone to the grocery store to get them some lunch. Callie let him in. She found their motel meals nerve-racking. With their fast-dwindling funds, they couldn't afford restaurants.

When she opened the door, Ian bowed and extended a small bouquet of daisies. "We met exactly one week ago today. Happy anniversary."

Callie gaped in disbelief. "You bought me flowers?"

He chuckled. "Good heavens, Callie! From the look on your face, you'd think no one had ever given you flowers."

"No one ever has," Callie said as she tentatively accepted the bouquet.

"No one?" Ian asked, incredulous.

Callie glanced up defensively from the flowers. The fight went right out of her at the expression on his face. It certainly wasn't pity she saw there. She didn't dare allow herself to acknowledge the emotion. It matched too closely her own feelings for him—feelings that she *had* to ignore.

"Has anyone given you a box of candy?" he asked. She shook her head. "How about a valentine?"

She gave him a smile, hoping it looked sincere. "Hey, Sherlock! Lots of girls go through life without hearts and flowers. Uncle Quincy and I were never in one spot long enough for some poor sucker to develop a crush on me."

Ian perceived the vulnerability reflected in her eyes, and his heart went out to her. He wanted to ask why Steven had never given her hearts and flowers, but the question would be cruel. He suppressed the urge to hug her. Any attempt to comfort her could backfire on him. Keeping his hands off her for the past five days had been the most difficult task he'd ever undertaken. His resolve was weakening with each passing moment.

Maintaining his distance was vital. Despite the progress he'd made with her during the past week, Callie didn't trust him. Not that he blamed her. She hadn't had much luck in the trust department. It was going to take time for her to accept that he would never deliberately hurt her.

"While you put those posies in water, I'll whip us up some ham on rye topped with a little Swiss cheese," he said, keeping the conversation light.

"My, we're becoming quite the gourmet, aren't we?" she teased, adding some levity to the scene to disguise her sudden shyness.

"Hey, if you've got it, you might as well flaunt it," he replied with a grin as he emptied the small grocery bag he'd brought in on her dresser.

Boy, does he have it! Callie thought as she took in the breadth of his shoulders, the length of his well-muscled legs and every other inch of his gorgeous body.

Noticing her scrutiny, he asked, "Something wrong?"

"No," she lied. Everything was wrong. Quincy remained maddeningly elusive, prison threatened for both of them, and all she could think about was how badly she wanted Ian. Fearing that her desire might be reflected in her eyes, she lowered them and said, "I'd better put these in water."

Ian studied her as she walked toward the bathroom. Clearly something was bothering her. What was he supposed to do if she refused to confide in him?

By the time Callie returned, Ian had made the sandwiches and handed her one. They sat down on the edge of the bed, keeping enough distance between them to make any physical contact impossible.

"I was thinking while you were gone," Callie announced when half of her sandwich was gone.

Ian smiled teasingly. "Sounds painful."

Callie grinned. "It was painless, but provocative."

"Oooh. I like the sound of that," he crooned.

Callie rolled her eyes in mock disgust. "Not *that* kind of provocative."

"Aw, shucks." He took another bite of his sandwich. "So, what were you thinking about that was so provocative?"

Callie kicked off her shoes and sat cross-legged on the bed. "We haven't run across any of Uncle Quincy's close friends."

"Is that significant? You said most of them were on the move continuously."

"They are, but I *should* have run across someone by now. We've been on the road nearly a week."

Ian reflected that in some ways it seemed as if he and Callie had met only yesterday; in other ways it seemed as if they'd been together forever. Again, he found himself studying her face. This time he didn't ignore the urge to touch her. He caught the tiny crumb of bread nestled in the corner of her mouth and brought it to his lips.

Callie stiffened at his touch. Mesmerized, she watched as he moved his fingertip to his mouth. She clenched her hands into fists to prevent herself from reaching out to caress the outline of his lips.

"What conclusion did you reach?" Ian asked, his voice low and gravelly. He knew she wanted him. And he wanted her. Lord, did he want her! But he wasn't going to succumb. They needed time to get to know each other, and she needed time to learn to trust him.

"There must be something going on that's luring everyone," she answered. "It's the only reason I can think of why we haven't made any contact with any of Uncle Quincy's friends."

"Like what?" Ian questioned as he ran the back of his thumb over his lower lip.

Callie lost track of the conversation as she fixed her gaze on his mouth. It was such a sexy mouth. So full and sensual. So . . .

"Callie . . ."

"What?" she whispered as she slowly raised her eyes to his.

"Stop staring at me like that."

"Like what?"

"Like you'd like to eat me up."

"I *would* like to eat you up."

He closed his eyes. "I'm not going to kiss you."

"Why?"

He opened his eyes and shook his head. "It isn't time for that. I *do* want to kiss you, you *know!*"

"So what's stopping you?"

"Would you believe a little angel on my shoulder?"

"Yes," Callie said with a wistful sigh. "Too bad you're not listening to the devil on the other shoulder."

"Oh, I'm listening." He caught her chin, drawing her face close. When his lips were no more than a pucker away, he added, "I'm just ignoring him." He released her. "What could be going on to keep Quincy's friends out of sight?"

She shrugged. "Anything from a big game to a birthday party. I'll ask some questions tonight at the pool hall and see what I come up with."

Damn! She dressed in baggy clothes when they were alone, but when they were on the prowl for Quincy, the look was hot and provocative. He was finding it harder and harder to control the itch to beat the daylights out of any man who even glanced at her in a pool hall.

Feeling possessive and jealous, all he wanted to do was throw her down on the bed and claim her.

Knowing that if he stayed in her room, he might do exactly that, he rose to his feet and said, "Well, I should get back to my room and grab a quick nap so I'll be fresh for tonight."

Callie nodded, though she didn't want him to leave. She wanted him to stay so they could talk. So they could kiss. So they could . . .

When he was gone, she lay down on the bed and gave her imagination full rein. She imagined Ian kissing her, making love to her. And heaven help her! She imagined herself falling in love with him!

QUINCY WAS TERRIFIED—it was time to begin the final stage of the hustle. He stuffed his hands into his pockets to stop their shaking. Then he moved over to the window of his motel room and looked at the Pot O' Gold Billiards Room, located across the street. The building was so dilapidated that he wondered why he'd always remembered it as a gleaming hall.

He'd won his first game against a pro at the Pot O' Gold. When he finally walked through its doors again, he would fulfill his vow to give up pool and settle down.

The thought of settling down brought Lucy to mind, and his lips curved into a smile. Lucy, the love of his life. Lucy, who understood him as no other could. Lucy, who'd handed him his freedom and then sat back to wait for him.

She wasn't the most gorgeous woman in the world, he admitted. Most people wouldn't even describe her as attractive. *They* didn't see beyond the outside package and into her soul, though. She was gentle and kind and generous. He'd never seen her lose her temper. He'd never heard her speak an unkind word. She loved him unconditionally. That knowledge brought tears to his eyes. If he got out of this mess alive, he was going to retire from pool and settle down with Lucy.

He considered calling Lucy and giving her the news. He'd better wait until it was all over. His hands were no longer shaking as he picked up the phone and dialed a number. Amazing how a little self-analysis could calm the nerves.

"Yeah?" a gruff voice muttered in his ear.

"It's McKiernan," Quincy said. "I'm ready to deal. Just to prove to you that I've got the ledgers, I've copied some of the pages. You can pick them up in a small pool parlor called Highpockets in Hanover. The package is in the men's room behind the mirror. Tell the boss I'll be in touch again soon to tell him how much it's going to cost him to get the books back."

He didn't wait for a response, loudly dropping the receiver into place. Who would ever have thought that he'd not only be playing cops and robbers, but that he'd be one of the good guys? Not that he'd ever been a bad guy, of course. He was just one of the shady characters who straddled a fine line. In this instance, he'd crossed the line because Lincoln Galloway had been forced into the car-theft ring by death threats against his family.

How could anyone consider making money off stolen cars to be worth more than a human life? For that matter, he couldn't think of anything on God's green earth that was worth taking someone's life.

Time to call Devon and let him know the bait had been cast. He picked up the phone receiver, speculating on whether it was safe to let Devon keep a lookout for the person making the pickup. Quincy wanted to be able to identify everyone involved in the hustle. Still, he was worried about Devon. The people they were dealing with were dangerous. He had confiscated Devon's trench coat, but he wouldn't put it past his friend to come up with another conspicuous "disguise."

He dialed the number for Highpockets and asked for Devon.

"McKiernan?" Devon gasped breathlessly when he came on the line.

"Dammit, Devon, this time we *aren't* supposed to be using names. You're in a room full of people who could overhear you. Where in the world is your head?"

"Callie's here, and she's—damn, and double damn! She's spotted me. You'd better call back. Gotta go."

"Devon!" Quincy bellowed. The line went dead.

Quincy pulled the receiver away from his ear and stared at it in disbelief. Devon didn't know to watch for the pickup, and if Callie was there, Quincy knew he didn't dare call back and tell him to keep his eyes open.

He hung up, collapsed on the bed and buried his head in his hands. The hustle had just begun, and already it was going wrong. What in the world was he going to do?

"WE'VE HIT PAY DIRT, Ian," Callie announced when they entered Highpockets. "One of Uncle Quincy's oldest and dearest friends is here."

"Where?" Ian asked with a sigh of relief. Already half a dozen men were staring at her. He had a feeling that if they didn't find Quincy soon, he'd be going to jail for a crime he *would* be guilty of—assault with intent to kill.

"He's over at the bar," she said with amusement. "The man in the cowboy suit."

Ian turned and stared at the man in openmouthed astonishment. He was dressed all in white from his cowboy hat down to his boots. "Good heavens, I haven't seen anything like him since the old Westerns I watched as a kid. Does he always dress like that?"

"No, but Devon is...different," she explained. "He's also extremely shy. Wait here while I talk to him."

Without waiting for a reply, she went over to the bar. "Devon, how are you?"

"Fit as a fiddle," he answered with an abashed duck of his head. "It's such a surprise to see you, Callie."

Callie smiled at him fondly. While Quincy considered Devon a simpleton, Callie regarded him as extremely intelligent. Unfortunately he was painfully introverted. His inability to communicate with people led them to label him a misfit. But the pool hustlers on the circuit accepted him and liked to have him around.

"You look great, Devon," she told him. "What have you been doing with yourself?"

"This and that. You?"

Callie sat on the bar stool next to him. "The action on the circuit is slow. Where is everyone?"

"Working their way toward Carlisle," he replied as he toyed with the fringe of his shirtsleeve. "There's a high-stakes tournament pulling together at a private home. It's promising to be a propitious event for every pool player who attends. Surprised you haven't heard about it. It's an open invitation if you've got the minimum."

Callie let out a whistle. A private game of that magnitude was rare. "What's the minimum?"

"Five."

"I guess high stakes is right. I bet Uncle Quincy let out a whoop when he heard about it."

"I wouldn't know," Devon responded, stiffly turning his head away from her.

Devon was lying to her and she knew it. He had actually spoken a full sentence without at least two words beginning with matching consonants or vowels! Did that mean Quincy would be at the game? She didn't bother to ask. If Quincy had asked him to keep it a secret, Devon would go to the rack before revealing the truth. Besides, if Quincy could come up with the stake, he'd be there. He loved private games because of all the free food and booze.

That meant she would have to come up with five hundred dollars if she was going to get into the game to find him. She'd have to hustle to get that much money. She observed Ian, who was standing on the fringes of a crowd watching a pool game. He had been the perfect gentleman during the past several days. Now, his patience would be severely tested by her announcement that she was going to hustle. She knew he wouldn't take well to that at all.

"When's this game supposed to take place?"

"At two, tomorrow."

Tomorrow? she wailed inwardly. There was no way she could come up with a five-hundred-dollar stake in that short a time. She'd never been one to give up that easily, though—where there were pool players, there was money. "Who's the top stick?" she questioned, studying the players in the room.

"The lad in the back left corner," Devon replied.

Callie eyed the man shooting at the back of the room. Surrounded by several women, he was clearly heart-throb material. He was playing up to them. Her interest stirred at the possibilities.

"Is he any good?"

"He has a moneyman."

Good. A backer to cover his bets—he would definitely suit her needs. The question was, how much of his strut was show, and how much of it was ego?

The only way to find out for certain was to approach him, and she regarded Ian. Simultaneously he glanced toward her and smiled. She felt the smile right down to the tips of her toes. Smiling back, she started working on a plan to get rid of him so she could feel out the stick.

"Devon, I need you to do a big favor for me."

"A favor for you?" he repeated cautiously.

Callie swiveled around on the bar stool and gave him her best coaxing smile. "I want to play a few games, but I have a new boyfriend who gets easily bored. Would you take him to dinner for me? It would be my treat, of course."

"Take him to dinner?" Devon repeated as he began to tug nervously on the cuff of his shirt.

"Please, Devon. You'll enjoy his company. It would mean a lot to me."

He focused nervously on the phone. "I can't, Callie. Someone's supposed to call me. I must remain right here."

"Devon, please," Callie cajoled. "Just for an hour. I'm sure the bartender will be glad to take a message for you."

"No!" he exclaimed in alarm. "No messages for me!"

"Devon, what's wrong? Are you in some kind of trouble?"

"No. I'm perfect as a peach," he answered quickly—too quickly for her peace of mind.

The phone rang at that moment. Devon nearly fell off the stool. His face drained of color when the bartender answered it. Something was definitely wrong with him. Callie grew even more determined to send him to dinner with Ian. Devon was in some kind of trouble, and maybe Ian could get to the bottom of it. After all, he'd dragged her entire life story out of her in one day.

When the bartender hung up, Devon gulped and smiled weakly. "Dinner sounds super, after all."

"Are you sure?" Callie asked. "I don't want you to miss your call."

"I have an hour to kill," he told her.

"Okay. I'll get my boyfriend and be right back."

He nodded. Callie slid off the stool, gnawing on her bottom lip as she moved toward Ian. Her initial plan had been to suggest Ian take Devon to dinner and pump him for information he'd been reluctant to tell her because she was Quincy's niece. Her next plan had been to appeal to the humanitarian in him by asking him to help Devon out.

"Well?" Ian asked when she reached him.

Callie drew in a deep breath. "There's going to be a private tournament in Carlisle tomorrow. It looks like Uncle Quincy will be there."

"Great. If we leave right away, we can be in Carlisle in a couple of hours." He grabbed her elbow and headed toward the entrance.

"Wait, Ian," she said, tugging on his shirtsleeve to make him stop. "I need a favor from you."

"What kind of favor?" he demanded warily, stopping in front of the door.

"Devon's in some kind of trouble. He won't talk to me. Could you take him to dinner and see if he'll talk to you?"

Ian grimaced. "You want me to play Tonto and take the Lone Ranger to dinner?"

"Please, Ian," she coaxed. "Devon is such a sweet soul. If I leave and something happens to him, I'll never forgive myself. All I need to know is if something is wrong. Then I'll call Mick, and he'll send in the cavalry. Just take him to dinner. It won't take more than an hour."

"What do you plan on doing while I'm at dinner?" he asked skeptically.

"I'll hang around. Watch the action," she answered nonchalantly.

Ian gazed down at her. She looked too innocent— some type of skulduggery was in motion. But she'd sounded genuinely concerned about her friend. The way the man was pulling on the fringes of his shirt convinced Ian that something was troubling him.

"Okay, Callie. I'll take your friend to dinner."

She impulsively threw her arms around his neck and hugged him. "Thank you, Ian."

"Yeah," he muttered gruffly. Her innocent shows of affection were far more devastating than her purposely seductive ones. "Let's go get your friend."

When Callie introduced him to Devon, Ian was stunned by the man's idiosyncratic speech. Dinner should be quite an interesting experience. He dropped a quick kiss to Callie's lips and murmured, "Stay out of trouble while I'm gone."

She batted her eyes at him. "Why, Ian, staying out of trouble is my specialty."

He shook his head mockingly, then followed Devon out of the pool hall.

Callie headed toward her quarry. The money she had on her wasn't enough to qualify as pocket change in the game she was looking to play. Fortunately she had a solid reputation on the circuit. Probably the backer would let her play on an I.O.U. If she lost, she'd be obliged to give him every penny she had on her toward the debt, leaving her and Ian dead broke. She didn't want to contemplate Ian's reaction to that.

9

CALLIE OPENED another button on her blouse as she strutted toward the stick's table. Either he'd take his time checking her out or he wouldn't be able to stand the tantalizing tease. She crowed in triumph when he immediately swung his head toward her. A stick with an *ego!*

"Hello, there," he murmured as his eyes traveled avidly down her body. "I haven't seen you around here before."

"Just traveling through," Callie answered, toying with the fine silver chain around her neck. The gesture had the effect she wanted. His eyes gravitated to her neckline and stayed. "I've been watching you play. You've very good."

"You an expert?" His leer indicated he wasn't necessarily talking about pool.

Callie ignored his innuendo and let her gaze slide to the table. "Expert enough to know I can beat you at nine ball."

He hooted in disbelief. "Honey, I haven't been beaten by a woman yet."

"Well, as they say, there's a first time for everything."

He appraised her. "You got a name?"

"Watson. Doc Watson."

When his eyes widened in surprise, Callie saw she had him hooked. Her reputation had preceded her.

"Interested in playing a couple of games?" he asked.

"I'm interested. Right now, I'm afraid I'm short of cash. So maybe the next time I'm in town." She moved toward the door.

"Hey, I think something could be worked out," he said, following her. "Why don't we talk about it?"

She glanced over her shoulder and shook her head. "I don't think so."

"Afraid you might get stuck with an I.O.U.?" he taunted.

"No," she replied. "I'm afraid I might end up carrying an I.O.U., and I'm already short of cash."

"I have a backer. Why don't I give him a call and see what we can arrange?"

Callie hesitated just long enough to make him nervously wet his lips. He was starving for the competition. Was he inexperienced enough that his hunger would make him reckless? Or would it heighten his skill? She couldn't read him well enough to tell. This time her hesitation was real.

But without a stake, she couldn't get into tomorrow's game. That meant she probably wouldn't be able to find Quincy. He could slip in and out of places like a ghost. She was going to have to take a chance on earning her stake here and pray that she didn't lose her shirt.

"Make your call."

BY THE TIME Ian returned to Highpockets, he felt just like Alice had after she'd attended the Mad Hatter's tea party. If he hadn't been certain that Devon Halloran was incapable of guile, he'd have sworn the man had been double-talking him. He'd also reached the conclusion that if Devon was in trouble, he wasn't about to confide in him about it.

He glanced around the room and frowned when he didn't see Callie. Though he didn't panic because he knew she wouldn't desert him, he couldn't restrain his feelings of suspicion. When she'd told him she'd just hang around and watch the action, he'd sensed something was up. Whatever it was, he felt he wasn't going to like it.

Devon went back to the bar, and Ian followed him. He caught the bartender's eye and asked, "I'm looking for my friend. Her name's Doc and she's a blonde about so high." He held his hand at chin level.

The bartender nodded. "She's in the back room. She said to tell you to have a beer and cool your heels."

Ian's stomach began to churn. "What's going on in the back room?"

"Private game," the bartender replied as he grabbed a beer mug.

"A private *pool* game?" Ian questioned.

"Well, we don't play bridge here," the man said. He filled the mug from the tap and slid it toward Ian. "It's already paid for."

Ian grabbed the mug and headed for the back room. A burly bruiser stepped in front of him before he reached the door. "There's a private game going on."

"My friend's in there," Ian told him. "I'm supposed to join her."

The man shook his head. "No one goes in after the game starts."

Ian determined that he was outmuscled. He returned to the bar, sitting at the opposite end from Devon. He wasn't in the mood for any more nonsensical conversation.

Staring down at the foam in his glass, he started to fume. Callie wasn't in there as a spectator. She was hustling! Damn! Why'd he let her talk him into taking Devon to dinner? And why was she hustling in the first place? They were running short of money, but weren't broke yet.

Then he remembered the excited gleam that appeared in her eyes each time they entered a pool hall. She just couldn't resist the lure of the tables. Recognizing that he'd object to her hustling, she'd trotted him off to dinner with Devon so she could do as she pleased.

He resigned himself to the situation. After all, he wanted her more than he'd ever wanted a woman. Botanist or pool hustler—he'd just have to accept her as she was.

The thought was depressing. He silently toasted Lucy Coates and her devotion to Quincy. Then, downing his beer in one gulp, he asked for another. When he reached for his wallet, the bartender shook his head. "This one's taken care of, too."

The realization that Callie had arranged for a bar tab to keep him occupied angered him. His anger intensified as he envisioned her playing. Just the thought that she'd be encouraging some stick to peer down her blouse made him contemplate storming the door—despite the "incredible hulk" guarding it. Had he been able to deck the hulk, Callie would in all probability then deck him. Any progress he'd made with her would be canceled out.

He finished off his beer. When the bartender nodded questioningly toward his empty glass, he shook his head. He didn't need another drink. He needed to think, and he rose to his feet and strode purposefully toward the door. A little fresh air might help him put this in perspective.

Outside, he closed his eyes and drew in a deep breath. Could Callie ever give up pool and settle down? What if the thrill of hustling had become a true addiction? He wanted an ordinary family life. Having a pool hustler for a wife was not ordinary.

Wife? Good heavens! That was rushing things. He'd only known her for a week and—

His thoughts were interrupted when Devon rushed out of the pool hall, nearly crashing into him. "Devon, what's wrong?" he asked with concern, noting the panic on his face.

"It's gone!" Devon exclaimed. "It's gone!"

"What's gone?"

Devon gave a frantic shake of his head. "When he called I should have known he'd told them to show up. I wasn't there to see who, and now it's gone! He'll shoot me for sure, this time. He'll shoot me for sure." He then dashed down the street.

"What in hell was that all about?" Ian muttered, watching Devon disappear from view. Now he *needed* another beer—and to do some serious thinking about his relationship with Callie. It was as good a time as any.

LOOKING DOWN at her watch, Callie cursed. The match had been going on for three hours. She and Romeo—as her opponent was aptly nicknamed—were running neck and neck. By now, Ian would be furious, but she couldn't think about that.

She'd badly underestimated Romeo. Callie had realized—too late—that the man was used to performing in the company of sexy women, so her "many charms" weren't breaking his concentration. She'd have buttoned up her blouse all the way to her neck—had she not believed that by doing so she'd reveal her nervousness to him.

She frowned at the two balls left on the table. One hung a half inch off the point of the side pocket and was in direct line with her cue ball. Unfortunately, the other ball was in the center at the end of the table. In order to sink both, she was going to have to use the complicated hook shot. The cue ball had to sink the first ball. Then, deflecting off the cushion, it had to hook out and run diagonally down the table, stopping in position to sink the final ball. At home, she always made the shot. Nevertheless she'd only used it twice professionally, and if it didn't work, she might as well go home. Romeo was ahead of her in money. If she lost this game, his lead would triple. She'd never catch up with him should that happen.

She glanced toward the backer who was sitting in the corner. She'd seen more animated mannequins. She'd never met him but knew him by reputation. He only worked with the best. He had a knack for finding unknown talent and grooming them for the circuit. He was also known for being amenable to reckless bets.

She drew in a deep breath and decided to go for the whole enchilada.

"I have a friend waiting for me," she announced, "and I can't keep him waiting much longer. How about if we play for double or nothing on these last two shots?"

"Double or nothing?" Romeo repeated with a laugh. "Do you always give your money away?"

Callie didn't even look at him. She continued to watch the backer, hoping to read something in his expression. If he went for the bet and she won, she'd walk out with her stake and more. If she lost, she'd walk out with empty pockets and Ian would probably shoot her.

Finally the backer nodded his assent. Callie returned her attention to the balls, resisting the urge to nervously rub her hand against her thigh.

You can do it! You've done it at home a hundred times. Performing in the privacy of her own home wasn't, however, the same as doing it for money. Her nerves were taut as she bent over the table.

She made the shot. Afraid to see if the cue ball had performed as it should, she closed her eyes for a second. Cracking one eye open, she watched the ball roll into perfect position.

"I'll be damned!" Romeo exclaimed in appreciation. Callie was pleased to see that there wasn't one ounce of hostility in his expression. Pool hustlers were ruthlessly competitive, but they were also generally good sports. She made the last shot with ease and collapsed against the table in relief. The backer handed her her money and left without a word.

Romeo flashed her a wide grin. "Well, Doc, you're as good as they say you are. How about shooting a few games just for the fun of it?"

Callie shook her head as she stored her cue stick in its leather case. It was the first time she'd used it since she and Ian had gone on the run. She ran her hand lovingly over its smooth wooden surface before closing the lid. "I really do have someone waiting for me. We were supposed to be headed out of town hours ago. He's probably ready to skin me alive."

Romeo wrapped a companionable arm around her shoulders and walked her out of the room. "Want me to play bodyguard?"

Callie laughed lightly and shook her head. "I think I can handle him. Thanks for the match. You really are good."

"Well, I expect a rematch the next time you're in town."

"You've got it," Callie promised.

She glanced around the room searching for Ian. When their eyes connected, she grimaced. His icy look disclosed he was *furious* just as she'd anticipated. The glare he fired at her companion shocked her. Good heavens! He was jealous! That was ridiculous! She moved from under Romeo's arm and told him good-bye.

"Ready to go?" she asked with a smile upon reaching Ian.

He ignored her question, dropping his gaze to the front of her blouse. "Why didn't you just take it off?" he said sarcastically.

"What makes you think I didn't?" Something dark and dangerous flashed through Ian's eyes, and Callie shivered. She ignored his ill-humor and asked, "Where's Devon?"

"He left hours ago."

"Did you find out what was wrong with him?"

"Other than he's got a few loose marbles, no." Ian rose to his feet slowly, and Callie cautiously tilted her head back as he straightened above her. His dominating position made her shiver again.

"I know you're mad at me, Ian," she told him. "But I do have a perfectly reasonable explanation."

"Oh, I'm sure you do," he drawled so softly that Callie gulped. "Are you sure you're ready to leave? Perhaps there's someone else here you'd like to stiff?"

"Drop dead," she snapped, stung by his words. She stalked toward the door.

"You should be so lucky," he growled as he fell into step beside her and took hold of her arm.

"What does that mean?" she demanded, attempting to jerk free of his hold. "Are you threatening me?"

He tightened his grip and scowled at her. "Probably."

His answer left her momentarily stunned. He propelled her out the door and to the car. Despite his threat, Ian would never hurt her—violence wasn't part of his makeup.

"What I did in there was for you," she explained.

"Sure."

"It's true."

"Sure."

He opened the passenger door and pushed her into the seat. She barely managed to draw her feet inside before the door slammed shut. When he slid in beside her, she cleared her throat before cautiously asking, "Uh, Ian, how much beer did you drink?"

"I'm not drunk, if that's what you're suggesting."

"I'm not suggesting anything. I'm merely asking a question."

"Yeah. Fasten your seat belt."

Callie hesitated at the order. Should she pursue the issue? He certainly didn't look intoxicated, but appearances could be deceptive. Quincy could look as sober as a judge and be falling-down drunk.

As she continued to stare at him, Ian cursed, then reached for her. When his lips came down on hers, they were raw and punishing, but Callie didn't fight him. She could sense that underlying the anger was desperation. She responded by circling her arms around him and stroking his back soothingly. Within moments, his kiss gentled and he trembled beneath her hands.

"You're driving me crazy," he whispered harshly as he broke away from the kiss. He cradled her head against his chest. "Absolutely crazy. And I can't stand it, Callie. For hours I sat in there thinking about that man peering down the front of your blouse. Then I saw him with his arm around you. I wanted to beat him to a pulp."

"That would have been a rather radical punishment for the crime," she noted softly.

Ian caught her chin and tilted her head upward. He frowned at her. "You really don't understand, do you?" He didn't wait for a response, but eased her back into her seat and said, "Buckle up. For your information, I've been drinking coffee for the past two hours."

"No wonder you're so uptight," she joked, trying to ease the tension in the car. "Don't you know that that much caffeine is bad for you?"

He opened his mouth as if to say something, but then closed it and shook his head. "What were you doing in there?"

"I'll tell you about it on the way to the motel. We need to pick up our things and get on the road."

Ian pulled into traffic, and Callie started talking. He was so absorbed in what she was saying that he didn't see the car that pulled out behind them.

"WELL, AT LEAST YOU did something right," Quincy grumbled at Devon when Callie and Ian left the motel and took the road to Carlisle. "It looks as if they're headed for the private game."

"I told you that I threw her a red herring and she took the bait," Devon stated truculently.

"Yeah," Quincy muttered as he made a U-turn and headed back the way they'd come. He tapped his fingers against the steering wheel. Maybe he should report Callie and Ian to the police again. Today they'd gotten too close for comfort. Now that he was in the final stage of the hustle, he couldn't afford to have them underfoot.

After seeing Callie, though, he knew he couldn't turn her in. Devon had bought him some time by sending her to Carlisle. Besides, it was apparent that she hadn't decoded the message he'd left on her answering machine.

The chances of her finding him before the hustle was over were slim.

"So what will we do now?" Devon asked.

Quincy shrugged. "We're going to stick to the plan and let the big boss sweat."

"I think it's time to involve the police," Devon said.

"Are you crazy? We can't trust the police to handle this. The big boss has Lincoln set up to take the fall. If the police screw up, they won't bother looking for the real crook because they'll have their case made with false evidence."

Devon gave a worried shake of his head. "I still think we should go to the police. I have a bad feeling about this, Quincy, and I've had it ever since Callie walked into Highpockets."

Quincy gaped at his friend in disbelief. "My word, man, you just spoke like a normal person. Are you sick?"

"No," Devon answered softly. "I always talk normally when I'm scared. Right now, I'm scared to death, Quincy."

"Me, too," Quincy murmured with a heartfelt sigh. "Only a fool wouldn't be scared."

IAN WAS SITTING on Callie's bed and stewing. He wanted to go with her to the private tournament. She insisted he stay behind. Her reason was that the men generally wore formal clothes and they couldn't afford to rent him a tux. Even had they been able to afford it, she'd have found another excuse to leave him behind.

He glowered at the brown leather box that contained her personal cue stick. Last night had been the first time she'd used it since they'd gone on the run. He resented its presence because it was a tangible reminder of her life-style. He also had this ominous feeling about it.

"Well, Ian, what do you think?" Callie asked, interrupting his troubling thoughts as she pirouetted out of the bathroom.

Ian's senses exploded as he stared at her. The two-piece outfit consisted of a form-fitting, strapless white bustier that molded to her body, zipped down the front and was smocked in the back. The matching white skirt was pencil thin and clung to her like a second skin. He wanted to throw her on the bed and make passionate love to her. He also wanted to turn her over his knee and paddle some sense into her.

"Why do you do this, Callie? You can win without the outrageous clothes."

Callie heard the underlying censure in his tone and bristled. "Perhaps you're right, Ian. But then I don't tell you how to run your business. Don't tell me how to run my career."

"*Career?*" he repeated disparagingly. "You're a pool hustler. That's not a career."

Glaring at him, she grabbed her purse, removing the money she'd won the night before. She counted out what she needed for her stake and tossed the remainder of it to him. "Hold on to that. That's our living expenses in case I don't find Uncle Quincy today."

Ian cursed when she stuffed the rest of the money into her bosom, grabbed her cue stick and went toward the door. He caught her arm, swinging her around to face him. "You are the most maddening woman I have ever met. When are you going to grow up?"

"Never!" she retorted as she jerked her arm out of his grip. "And I'm sick and tired of listening to your lectures. If you want to play boss, then get married and have a couple of kids. I'm told they respond well to authority." With that, she slammed the door behind her.

"Someday I'm going to give you a taste of your own medicine," Ian vowed angrily. His eyes latched on to the crumpled money in his hand. Suddenly he knew *exactly* how he was going to do it. But first, he had to make a call to his father.

CALLIE WANDERED OUT onto the patio of the private mansion, smiling and waving at friends at the far end. It was midafternoon, and the sun warmed her bare shoulders. She didn't dare stay out too long or she'd sunburn. Considering that Quincy loved the sunshine, she'd risk sunburn, certain that this was where she'd find him.

Working her way across the patio, she observed that the crowd was a mixture of pool players and "high society"—the term was not a compliment. They were people with money to burn and got their kicks by rubbing elbows with the hoi polloi. Callie despised their subtle and many times not-so-subtle putdowns—which was why she hadn't attended a party like this in years.

"I've been thinking about you a lot lately, Doc," a man said behind her, and Callie smiled when she turned and saw Dynamite Dan.

"Dynamite! How are you?"

"Just fine. By the looks of you, you're just fine yourself." His soft brown eyes conducted a quick survey of her attire, but there was nothing but friendship in his gaze. "A man was looking for you a week or so ago. Did he find you?"

Callie nodded. "He's an acquaintance of Uncle Quincy's."

"How is Quincy?" Dynamite asked. "I haven't seen him in ages."

"Neither have I," Callie admitted. "I was hoping he'd be here today so I could assure myself he's okay. You know how he is. He can get into trouble faster than a cage full of monkeys."

Dynamite chuckled and snagged a glass of champagne from the tray of a passing waiter. He offered it to Callie, but she shook her head.

Darn! She'd been sure Quincy would be here. But where was he? Maybe he was inside at the buffet table.

"I need to get out of the sun before I turn into a lobster," she told Dynamite. "I'll see you later."

Dynamite nodded. Before she could turn away from him, he said, "Hey, isn't that the guy we were just talking about?"

"What?" Callie looked around in confusion. Her mouth dropped open in shock. Ian was standing in the doorway leading out to the patio. He was dressed in a tuxedo, complete with black tie and ruffled shirt, and black tooled-leather cowboy boots.

Her pulse began to pound, and she gulped. The man was gorgeous to begin with; in formal clothes he was devastating!

She was gaping but couldn't help herself. What in the world was he doing here? And where in the world had he gotten the tux and the boots? Her eyes narrowed as she watched a high-society dame approach him. When the woman wrapped her hand around his upper arm and he smiled flirtatiously at her, Callie felt the urge to kill. Without being aware of what she was doing, she snatched a glass of champagne from a passing waiter. She gulped down half of it while watching the woman lead him toward a group of her female friends.

When Ian said something that made the group of women laugh, Callie gulped down the remainder of the champagne. And when another woman attached herself to him, Callie nearly broke the stem of her glass. The man was holding court! And she wanted to scratch his eyes out!

"It looks as if he has the routine down pat," Dynamite drawled. "I've always admired a man who knows how to work the ladies. It sure beats hustling pool, and it can be a heck of a lot more lucrative—not to mention the great benefits that come along with the job."

Dynamite's words only made Callie more furious. How dare Ian come here and make a spectacle of himself!

"See you later, Dynamite," she muttered as she plopped her empty glass on a table. She then strode toward Ian, determined to send him back to the motel where he belonged.

When Ian saw Callie approaching, he purposely ignored her. As soon as she was within hearing distance, he turned his full attention on the gorgeous redhead draped across his arm.

"I'm starving," he told her in a husky croon. "Why don't we visit the buffet table?"

She batted her eyelashes at him. "Why, darling, of course we'll visit the buffet table. Then we'll find someplace quiet where we can get to know each other."

Darling! Callie silently screeched as she listened to the exchange. She'd "darling" the woman, and if Ian so much as *tried* to find "someplace quiet where they could get to know each other," she'd strangle him!

He led the redhead into the house, but before Callie could catch up with them an old friend stopped her and asked where Quincy was.

"I don't know. I haven't seen him in weeks," she told the man, craning her neck to keep Ian in sight. She bit back a curse when he and the woman disappeared. Her attention was distracted from them when three more friends approached and asked about her uncle.

She frowned in concentration. It wouldn't be unusual for two or three people not to have seen Quincy, but it was becoming apparent that no one had seen him. That *was* unusual, and worrisome. Pool was to Quincy what work was to a workaholic. Where was he?

Her tooth began to ache, and she rubbed her jaw. Suppressing the overwhelming urge to follow Ian and his redhead, she made some inquiries about Quincy. Heaven help Ian if he was in a compromising position by the time she caught up with him. He was *hers*. And no high-society dame was going to take him away from her!

Callie stumbled and caught the back of a chair to keep from falling when that declaration registered.

Good heavens, she couldn't be in love with the man! She'd only known him a week, and—

But she was in love with him, and she knew it. She consoled herself with the reminder that love was a transitory emotion. With Steven, it had been a slow awakening of womanhood. With Ian it had been an instant reawakening. After all, she was a normal, healthy woman, and she and Ian had been forced into constant companionship. When they finally found Quincy and weren't together twenty-four hours a day, seven days a week, her desire would cool, as would her feelings. That's what had happened with Steven, anyhow.

No amount of rationalization could soothe her feeling of jealousy. She hurried toward a group of friends, determined to get her questioning over with so she could go looking for Ian.

10

WHERE IN HELL was Callie? Ian wondered as the red-head backed him into a corner and eyed him with the intensity of a bloodhound on the scent. He wasn't averse to an aggressive woman. Still, there was aggression, and then there was *aggression*.

Of course, if it had been Callie coming after him like this, he wouldn't be resisting. But this wasn't Callie. When the woman raked her long, painted fingernails down the front of his shirt, Ian's flesh recoiled. He placed his hands on her shoulders, ready to push her away. Then he saw Callie bearing down on them. The look in her eyes revealed her fury. He began to stroke the redhead's arm.

"Here you are, *darling*," Callie simpered when she reached Ian's side. "Have you taken your medicine? You know what the doctor said. You aren't going to get rid of that nasty little infection if you don't take your medicine faithfully."

"Infection?" the redhead repeated, warily backing away from him.

Callie smiled cheerfully at the woman. "Oh, don't worry, honey. Why, the doctor cleared me up in no time. You aren't allergic to penicillin, are you?"

"Oh, you must excuse me!" the woman exclaimed, panic evident in her face. "I just saw a friend I must speak with."

"Ta, ta," Callie stated brightly as the redhead rushed away.

"That was dirty pool," Ian muttered as he leaned against the wall.

Callie scowled at him. "You would have learned what dirty pool was if you'd gotten tangled up with her. What are you doing here?"

"Having a good time," he answered with a shrug. "Why should you have all the fun?"

"Fun?" Callie yelped. "I'm not having fun. I'm looking for Uncle Quincy!"

"Yeah. Have fun looking. I'm going to mingle."

Callie grasped his arm as he levered himself away from the wall. "You are *not* going to mingle. You're going back to the motel."

"Says who?"

"Says me. Dammit, Ian. Do you know what that woman thought you were?"

He tapped a finger against his lips as if giving her question considerable thought. "An interesting man?"

"That wasn't what she thought, and you know it," she railed. "What are you trying to prove?"

"Nothing. How do you like the tux?"

Callie's eyes dropped to his clothes and her toes curled—twice.

"Come on, Ian, you're getting out of here," she said, grabbing his arm. She could imagine only too well the effect he was having on all the rich, bored dames in the place.

"I'm not going anywhere," he replied as he easily detached himself from her grasp. "I told you, I'm here to have fun."

"Ian, if you don't leave right this minute, I swear I'll—"

"Hey, Doc! Your number's up," someone called from behind her.

Callie glanced over her shoulder in frustration. All the pool players had been assigned numbers when they'd arrived and been paired up with "high society" members for playoffs. The winners of each match would then be paired off until they finally worked their way down to the final two players. After speaking with Quincy's friends, Callie was convinced he wasn't going to show up. Nevertheless she'd already paid her money; it went against the grain for her to walk away from it.

She glanced back at Ian. "I have to go play. *You* stay out of trouble."

"Staying out of trouble is my specialty," he stated, using her own words from Highpockets the night before.

Callie turned away, cursing when he laughed softly behind her. When she got him back to the motel, she was going to skin him alive!

She soon discovered that she should have skinned him alive on the spot. Ian followed her into the pool room, and she couldn't concentrate on her game as she witnessed his peacock show. She may have scared off the redhead, but half a dozen other women had taken her place. Ian was playing them for all he was worth.

Callie seethed when he released his bow tie and unbuttoned the top button of his shirt while asking one of the women if she was as hot as he was. The double entendre was so blatant, and Callie was so furious with him, she missed her shot. Luckily the "high society" player she was paired with was inept, and she was quickly back in control of the table. As she readied herself for another shot, Ian's jacket came off and another button came undone. Good heavens, the man was doing a striptease!

She managed to retain enough concentration to sink the next two balls. Then Ian unfastened yet another button, baring enough of his hair-covered chest to be posing for a beefcake poster. She struck the cue ball so hard it followed her intended ball right into the pocket.

Callie stared at the pool table in horror. She'd scratched the cue ball. She hadn't done that since she was fifteen years old! She'd also lost the game, and her five hundred dollars was history. She was going to kill Ian!

She managed to politely congratulate her opponent. When she turned around to confront her nemesis, he was gone.

IAN GRABBED a glass of champagne. Settling down on a lounge chair by the pool, he waited for Callie to find him. He'd made a large dent in their living-expense fund by renting the tux and buying the boots, but he wasn't worried about it. When he'd called his father he'd asked him to wire him some money, and his father had promised it would be at Western Union in the morning. He didn't like involving his parents in this escapade, but he wasn't about to let Callie do any more hustling on his behalf. There came a time when a man must take control, and his time had come.

He watched the patio door. By now Callie was probably foaming at the mouth. When she finally appeared, his heart did somersaults—she was positively glorious in a rage. When she furiously swooped down on him, he bit his inner cheek to keep from bursting into laughter. He also had to shift his position in the chair so his erection wasn't evident.

"Where's your harem?" she said sarcastically.

"Harem?" Ian repeated with feigned obtuseness.

"The more appropriate term might be *stable*," she muttered, not attempting to veil her asperity.

Ian shrugged. "They're around." He let his gaze wander brazenly down her before baldly asking, "Why? Do you want to join my harem?"

She glared at him while considering the advantages of drowning him in the pool. "I'd rather eat worms."

Ian tossed back his head and roared with laughter. His eyes were dancing with devilry. "Make sure you use lots of horseradish. They go down a lot easier that way."

Callie didn't respond. Instead, she cast a withering look at his half-open shirt. "I'm convinced that Uncle Quincy has no intention of showing up today. If you're through making an exhibition of yourself, I suggest we leave."

Ian gazed pointedly at her delectable bosom. "Why, Dr. Watson, surely you aren't intimating that what's good enough for the goose isn't good enough for the gander?"

A hot blush suffused her face at his words. She tried to tell herself that it was anger. The truth was she felt as if he'd plunged a knife into her heart and then given it a twist. He'd deftly put her in her place, and he couldn't have done it better if he'd been a member of the "high society" dishing it out.

"Touché, Sherlock," she responded, glancing away from him to hide her hurt feelings. "As far as I'm concerned, the gander can do whatever he wants. This goose, however, is going home. Don't worry, though. I'm sure one of your doting admirers will be happy to give you a lift."

Ian cursed as she whirled around and walked off. He sprang out of the lounge chair. Heading after her, he realized that he'd carried his charade a step too far. He'd wanted to give her a taste of her own medicine—not overdose her with it. He owed her an apology.

He waited until they'd reached the car before he spoke. "Callie, I'm sorry about what I said back there. I was only teasing."

"Apology accepted," she replied stiffly, refusing to look at him.

Ian knew she was still offended. Although he was tempted to have it out with her right then and there, he resolved to wait until they got back to the motel.

The silent drive was pure torture for Callie. She felt an overpowering need to indulge herself in self-pity. Yet she hated feeling sorry for herself—all it did was make her miserable.

You are what you were born to be. The sooner you come to grips with it, the sooner it stops hurting.

She was tired of always having to accept the inevitable. She was tired of trying to come to grips with it. And she was tired of trying to convince herself that it didn't hurt, when actually it hurt like hell.

Thankfully she pulled into the parking lot of the motel before she'd managed to sink into a numbing depression. She climbed out of the car and strode toward her door without a single glance at Ian.

When she heard him coming up behind her, she was torn between the urge to run and the urge to yell at him, but she'd already made a big enough fool of herself today.

She lifted her room key, but she missed the lock. Ian placed his hand on her shoulder and murmured softly, "Callie, I really am sorry. Please, forgive me."

The contriteness in his voice hurt Callie more than his earlier gibe had, because what he'd said back at the mansion had been true. She had no right to be offended by it. "I already told you that your apology was accepted. Drop the subject, Ian."

When once again she tried to insert the key in the lock and missed, Ian took it away from her and opened the door. Callie realized he was going to follow her inside.

"You aren't going to leave this alone, are you?" she asked as she kicked off her shoes, sat down on the foot of her bed and began massaging the soles of her feet.

"No," Ian said with a heavy sigh as he closed the door and locked it. "I admit, I showed up at the mansion today to give you a sample of what it's like to watch you prance around pool halls dressed like a femme fatale, but I didn't mean to offend you. I was only trying to make a point."

"Well, you made it." She glanced up at him, and Ian's heart lurched because all her pretension was gone and her eyes were filled with tears. "I can't change what I am, any more than you can change what you are. When are you going to accept that?"

"Callie—" He took a step toward her.

She gave a weary sigh. "Please leave, Ian. I'd like to be alone."

He gave an exasperated shake of his head. "I'm not going to leave you alone when you're upset."

"Fine. Stay," she stated dully as she rose to her feet and padded to her suitcase. "I'm going to take a shower."

"No, you're not," Ian told her, his temper flaring. Two strides brought him to her and he grabbed her arms and spun her around to face him. "I hurt your feelings today, so scream at me or kick me or throw something at me, but do *something!*"

"And what would that solve?" Callie demanded with an angry toss of her head. She welcomed the fit of temper, because she had a feeling that without it, she'd dissolve into tears.

"It would make you feel better," Ian answered.

"It would make *me* feel better, or make *you* feel better?" she responded sharply. She broke away from his hold. "That's what's going on here. You have a guilty conscience. If I fight with you, you can appease it. Well, I'm not going to let you appease it. You behaved like a jerk, and by damn, you deserve to feel like one!"

"You are absolutely stunning when you're mad," Ian commented with a sexy grin. "Do you get turned on when you're mad, Callie?"

He'd asked the question in a husky voice that sent a bolt of desire streaking through her. It was so powerful that only pride kept her from rushing into his arms. "What kind of a question is that?"

"The most basic kind." He took a step toward her, and she took a step back. "I sure hope you get turned on when you're mad because I want to make love to you, Callie, and I want to do it now."

Callie took another step back, shaking her head. "I don't want you to touch me."

"Liar." He reached out and wrapped his hand around the back of her neck, pulling her nearer to him.

"Ian!" she whispered in breathless excitement.

He lowered his head and flicked his tongue across her bottom lip, making her groan. "Kiss me, Callie."

"No." But she stepped closer, nestling against him. She moaned softly when her hand touched the heavy mat of hair on his chest. He stared down at her, his eyes dark and smoky with desire. Yet she knew that as much as he wanted her, she was going to have to make the first move.

Callie told herself she had to pull away before this went any further. She told herself that if she made love with him, she'd only be further complicating their already complicated relationship. She told herself that nothing could ever last between them.

But passion won out. Her future looked so grim, and she wanted—*needed*—this time with Ian.

"Love me, Ian," she whispered, and sealed her lips over his.

Ian's heart raced. He didn't know if it was from the ardor of her kiss or those three simple words she'd spoken. *Love me, Ian.* And as crazy as it seemed, he did love her. *Could* she let him love her in the way she should be loved? Or was the lure of the tables too strong?

He caught her chin and raised her head, searching her eyes for answers, but they were unfathomable. Suddenly he was hit with a sense of urgency—his time with her was running out. He lowered his mouth to hers, groaning when she parted her lips and arched against

him. If time was his enemy, then he was going to fight
it with the only weapon he had left in his arsenal: he'd
hand her his heart and pray she didn't reject it.

Callie's breath caught in her throat when Ian stripped
her clothes from her, whispering, "Beautiful. You're so
damn beautiful." She shivered as his brilliant blue eyes
poured over her, then focused on the small scrap of
white satin and lace that clung to her hips. Fire raced
through her veins when he slid his hand between her
thighs and rocked his palm against her in an intimate
rhythm that stole the strength from her limbs.

Ian caught her when her knees buckled and swung
her up into his arms. He carried her to the bed. Callie
licked at her lips with anticipation as he pulled off his
clothes—his own need for her blatant and pulsing with
life.

She reached for him, but Ian shook his head as he
stripped her panties from her hips. Then he caught her
wrists in his hands and levered them over her head in a
grip as soft as silk but as unyielding as iron.

"I'm going to love you in the way that you should always be loved," he rasped as he straddled her and then
lowered his head to her breast.

Callie was sure she was going to pass out as he trailed
his tongue over her flesh, always coming close to, but
never connecting with her nipple.

"Ian, please!" she cried out passionately.

He ignored her plea and turned his attention to her
other breast. Callie moaned and moved restlessly beneath him, needing to touch him, but unable to free her
wrists from his hands.

Then he pulled her arms down to her sides and an-
chored them against the mattress as his lips began to

move lower, across her flat abdomen and down to her inner thighs. When his tongue finally touched her intimately, Callie could hardly bear it.

Again she struggled to free her wrists. This time he released her. She grasped his head and arched against him urgently. While his tongue continued its magic, he slid his hands up to her breasts, and Callie gasped as his fingers grazed her nipples. One more flick of his tongue sent her into oblivion.

She murmured in protest when he pulled away from her. She rolled to her side, stroking his back as he grabbed his pants, pulled out his wallet and retrieved a foil packet. His preparation was quick, and he was back in her arms, cradling her tenderly as he slid between her parted thighs.

"So beautiful," he whispered hoarsely as he entered her with a maddening slowness that had her close to climaxing.

"Just love me, Ian. Just...love...me," Callie gasped when he flexed his hips and surged into her, completing their union.

"I do love you, Callie," he said, and then caught her lips in a fiery kiss that didn't end until they'd both shuddered in release.

Callie could barely keep her eyes open when Ian finally rolled to his side. Her sleepiness vanished when he declared soberly, "I meant it, Callie. I'm in love with you."

She leaned her head back and sighed heavily when she saw the sincerity reflected in his face. She reached up and trailed her fingers along his jaw. Her first impulse was to deny his words. As she continued to regard him, she knew that denial wasn't the solution; honesty was. And she had to be honest with him.

"I know you do," she said. "But it isn't *love*, Ian." He parted his lips to protest, but she rested her fingers against them. "What's happening between us is occurring only because we're on the run. The fear of being caught has made life more immediate for us. When this is all over and your life is back to normal, your feelings for me will change."

"What you're saying is true," he conceded, "but only up to a point. Without the immediacy, it would probably have taken me months to acknowledge my feelings for you. I think I fell in love with you the moment I laid eyes on you."

When she opened her mouth to object, Ian stopped her with a kiss, then continued, "I know this has happened too fast for you, honey. I recognize it's going to take time for you to learn to trust me. But you will learn to trust me, Callie. I'm here for the duration."

"Oh, Ian, you don't know what you're saying," she said miserably. "Even if what you're feeling is love, it can't last. My past will always be there to haunt you. Love can't withstand that type of stress."

He tangled his fingers in her hair and looked into her eyes. "Love can survive anything, Callie. All you have to do is believe in it."

As Callie gazed into his beloved face, she saw he honestly believed what he was saying. She'd never be able to have the faith in love that he had. You were what you were born to be, and she simply hadn't been born into Ian's world. There was no way she'd ever be able to enter it—especially with her past. He might love her now. Eventually he'd come to despise her.

"We'll just continue to take it a day at a time and see what happens," she told him. It was easier to pacify him than argue with him.

Ian closed his eyes in resignation. She was protecting herself by distancing herself. He prayed that they'd soon find Quincy. Once they got their lives back on track, he could court Callie just as he'd court any other woman, and would prove to her that his love for her was real and lasting.

Callie waited until she knew Ian was asleep before she crept from bed. She pulled on her robe, went into the bathroom and sat on the edge of the bathtub to think. Ian's confession of love had rattled her more than she cared to admit. She knew that it was crucial that she find Quincy, because it was not just *her* heart she had to worry about; she also had to worry about Ian's.

After talking to Quincy's friends today and learning that he hadn't been seen in nearly two months, she had no idea where to look for him. The key to his whereabouts had to be in the message he'd left on her answering machine. However, no matter how hard she racked her brain, she couldn't figure out what he'd been trying to tell her.

"Are you okay?" Ian asked from the doorway, and Callie jerked her head toward him. Her heart skipped a beat when she saw him leaning against the door frame in unselfconscious nudity. He was so beautiful he brought tears to her eyes.

She shook her head in answer to his question. "No, I'm not okay. Uncle Quincy's disappeared off the face of the earth, and I'm worried sick about him. What if something's happened to him?" Her voice quavered. "He's all I've got, Ian, and I'll die if I lose him."

Ian pulled her up into his arms. "Nothing's happened to him, Callie. I promise you, nothing has happened to him."

"No one's seen him! And his message is utterly confusing. If I could understand it, I could find him."

"Then let's unravel it," Ian suggested as they left the bathroom. "Where's your tape player?"

"In my suitcase."

Ian settled her on the bed, retrieved her tape player and brought it to her. Then he sat down beside her. "When you play it this time, don't listen to the words, listen to his voice. Maybe you can pick up something from the inflection."

Callie nodded, pushed the Play button, closed her eyes and listened intently. When the tape was over, she gave a miserable shake of her head.

"It's there, Ian, but I can't get hold of it. What am I going to do?"

He tenderly smoothed her hair off her forehead. "What would you do if you didn't have the tape?"

"I don't know. Contact his friends, tell them I thought he was in trouble, and ask them to keep an eye out for him."

"Well, most of his friends are in town. Why don't you call them in the morning and tell them exactly that?"

She considered his suggestion, then nodded. "I'm going to do that, but we'll have to stay here instead of searching for Uncle Quincy. They'll need a way to reach me."

"Then we'll stay here. Now, come back to bed. I want to hold you," he told her huskily.

She glanced up at him with a teasing smile. "Is that all you want to do?"

"For now," he murmured with a low chuckle as he dropped a quick kiss to her lips. "Later—"

"Oh, I look forward to later," Callie whispered as she wrapped her arms around him and hugged him tightly, blinking against another surge of tears.

She knew she was in love with him, and it was real and deep and hopeless. If she'd only met him before she'd met Steven, maybe things could have turned out differently. But she hadn't met him before Steven, and there was no way she could change the past. All she could do was love him for now and hope that she wouldn't perish from heartbreak when she had to let him go.

11

"MMM," IAN HUMMED with pleasure as he gradually awakened. Callie was cuddled against him. He'd heard the position described as spoon-fashion—even spoons didn't fit together this nicely.

He smiled as he put his nose in her hair, inhaling its freshly shampooed fragrance. He wanted to make slow, leisurely love to her, but he didn't have any more protection. He'd have to make a quick trip to his room before he could savor every delicious inch of her.

Callie suddenly stretched and settled her bottom more firmly against him. Ian groaned at the exquisite sensation set off by her movement and he was instantly aroused. He kept telling himself to let her rest. That didn't stop his hand from gliding over the satin smoothness of her flat stomach or his fingers from tangling in the soft blond curls that covered her womanhood.

"Ian?" she murmured sleepily.

"Mm-hmm?" he whispered as he nuzzled her ear.

"You're aroused."

He chuckled and nibbled on her earlobe. "Why would you say that?"

"Well, you aren't wearing pants, so that can't be a banana in your pocket," she quipped as she raised her hand to her mouth and covered a yawn. Then she shifted to her back and smiled up at him. "Good morning."

"It's a wonderful morning."

"How about a kiss to prove it?"

"Just a kiss?"

"Can you think of any better place to start?"

"Honey," he said gruffly, "there are so many places I'd like to start that it's mind-boggling."

Thrilled by his arousal, Callie felt desire flow through her. She skimmed her fingers over his erection as she replied, "The feeling's mutual."

He chuckled again and she wrapped her arms around his neck and pulled him toward her. "I need a time-out," Ian answered reluctantly.

"Why?" Callie asked, hurt by his rejection.

"Don't pout." He dropped a quick kiss to her lips. "I need to go to my room and get a condom. It will only take a minute."

Callie nervously caught her lower lip between her teeth. "You don't need to worry about protection. I'm on the pill," she informed him.

His expression didn't waver. "Then I guess I won't need time-out."

"Don't you want to know why I'm on birth control?" she asked, knowing that she was pushing the issue but unable to help herself.

"No," he murmured with a loving smile.

Callie was amazed that he had so much faith in her sexual mores than he didn't even question them, but before she could think the issue through, he treated her to a kiss that left her head reeling, and she groaned when he rolled onto his back, pulling her over him. When his tongue teased for entrance into her mouth, she complied. She moaned as his hands slid down to her buttocks and pressed her hips. His manhood was hot and pulsing against her stomach, and she straddled him.

"Love me, Callie," he encouraged as he rained kisses from her forehead to her chin. "Love me, honey."

Callie raised her hips so he could enter her. His stroking of her sensitive flesh was nearly enough to send her over the edge. When he placed his hands on her hips and urged her onto him, she was certain she was going to come. She flexed her legs, ready to engulf him in an instant, but he held her back.

"Slowly, honey," he whispered hoarsely. "I don't want to hurt you, and you may not be ready for me yet."

Callie *was* ready for him but she enveloped him slowly, wanting to prolong the sensation.

"Oh, Callie!" Ian gasped as she took him into her, inch by torturous inch. He didn't miss the smile of satisfaction that curved her mouth. He dug his hands into the sheets and refused to let himself surge upward. This was her dance, and he was going to let her choreograph it—even if it took ten years off his life.

When she began to move, he stopped her. "Let me touch you."

He ran his hands down her slowly, teasing at her nipples, her navel, and finally pressed his fingers against the nucleus of her passion.

Her body tightened around him in response to his ministrations. Ian sucked in a harsh breath, unable to stop his hips from rising.

"Oh, Ian!" Callie gasped. She then lowered her head and kissed him as she began to move in a slow, undulating rhythm that provided them both with maximum pleasure.

Ian was certain he was going to explode as her taut nipples brushed tantalizingly against his chest and her hips rocked against his. She teased his ear with her tongue and whispered erotic words of love to him.

Then he took control of their lovemaking. He felt both arrogant and humble as he brought her toward release; he realized that only love could make it this good.

"It's time, honey," he rasped when he felt her body tighten around him again. "Let's do it together. Let's do it now, honey. Now!"

Callie cried out his name as he surged deeply into her. She clung to him as he shuddered with his own release. She'd never experienced anything so beautiful, and tears of rapture began to spill down her cheeks.

"Callie, what is it? Did I hurt you?" Ian whispered hoarsely as he began to kiss away her tears. "I'm sorry. I should have been more careful. I should have—"

"Shh," Callie interrupted as she pressed a soft kiss to his lips. "I'm not hurt. I'm happy. Very, very happy."

Her words brought the unaccustomed sting of tears to Ian's own eyes, and he tenderly brushed her bangs off her forehead. "I love you."

He could see his own feelings reflected in her face, but she didn't return his declaration of love. Instead she rubbed her hand lovingly against his beard-stubbled jaw and said, "As much as I'd like to stay in bed with you for the rest of the day, I'd better get up and start making some calls before everyone skips town."

Ian closed his eyes, refusing to let her lack of response hurt. It was going to take time for her to learn to trust him. The reward, however, would be worth the wait. He knew that when she was finally able to say she loved him, she'd belong to him forever.

He opened his eyes and dropped a quick kiss to her lips. "While you make your calls, I'm going to check out of my room. Then I'll go get us some breakfast."

For a moment Callie balked at his decision to move in with her. Considering how short of money they were, maintaining two rooms when Ian would be spending most of his time in hers would be absurd. Practical as his plan was, still she objected to it. The closer she let Ian get to her, the harder it was going to be to let him go.

Who was she trying to kid? He was already so close to her that when he left, he'd be taking her heart with him.

"QUINCY, THIS PLAN is insane!" Lincoln exclaimed. "You want to steal the mayor's car to catch a car thief?"

"Can you think of anyone else the police will crawl out of bed for? We have to fight fire with fire."

"You *are* nuts," Lincoln muttered as he collapsed on a nearby chair. "We should just go to the police and tell them what we know."

"My sentiments exactly," Devon stated from his spot in the far corner of the room. "This isn't a hustle, Quincy. It's suicide. If the bad guys don't get us, the police will."

Quincy shook his head vehemently. "They've framed you, Lincoln. If we can't catch them red-handed, then you're going to take the fall as the leader of the pack."

"Stealing the mayor's car is going to save my hide? No way, Quincy."

"First we're going to steal it and park it. Then we're going to make the big boss crawl into it and lead him on a merry chase. By the time he arrives at the books, we'll have alerted the police and they'll be waiting. He'll get stuck with all the goods. He'll be dead meat—one way or the other. Either he'll be charged with the car theft operation or for stealing the mayor's car."

Lincoln glanced at Devon. "What do you think?"

Devon shrugged. "It sounds crazy enough to work. But since you're the one they've set up, it should be your call."

Lincoln frowned in frustration. "You know that we're going to have to turn ourselves in when this is all over. We could still end up in jail."

"That's possible," Quincy admitted. "I'm willing to take the risk."

"And what about you, Devon?" Lincoln asked. "They could get you for aiding and abetting."

Devon shrugged again. "All my life I've lived on the outskirts of society—which is its own kind of prison. At least if I'm behind real bars, I'll be guaranteed clothes on my back and food in my mouth."

"So, what's your decision?" Quincy questioned as he studied Lincoln's face.

"I've managed to get my family out of town, so they're safe. I'm in," Lincoln acceded, sighing heavily.

"Devon?" Quincy asked. To his surprise, Devon seemed to have changed into a normal man overnight. It was a positive sign for Devon. Nonetheless it saddened Quincy because it signaled that nothing would ever be the same again when this hustle was over.

"I'm in," Devon said.

Quincy nodded. "According to the paper, the mayor's going to be out of town next weekend. That gives me an entire week to set up our plan. In the meantime, we're all going to lay low. We don't want to attract any attention."

WHEN IAN ENTERED the motel room and heard the shower running, he nodded with satisfaction. He'd timed his return perfectly. He hurried to prepare his surprise for Callie.

He deposited his packages on the small dresser. Then he pushed the bed up against the wall, pulled the blanket he'd retrieved from the car off his shoulder and spread it on the floor. Next, he opened one of the paper bags he'd carried in and pulled out the tapered candles and their holders. He set them on the blanket and lit them. The brightly colored paper plates and napkins were next. Then he unwrapped the two crystal wineglasses he'd splurged on.

He was able to get the wine open and the pizza box settled in the middle of the blanket by the time the shower turned off. Pulling two wrapped boxes from another paper bag, he quickly shoved them beneath the bed. Finally he rummaged through Callie's suitcase, found her tape player and popped in the tape whose title simply read, "Music to Make Love By." The opening strains of Beethoven's *Moonlight* Sonata filled the air. On cue, Callie stepped out of the bathroom, dressed in a soft rose velour robe that matched the high color in her cheeks.

"What in the world is all of this?" she asked.

"It's dinner, madam," Ian stated as he stepped forward with a bow. Then he took her hand and led her to the blanket. "If madam will sit, I'll serve the wine."

Stunned, Callie sat down. When Ian settled beside her and began to pour the wine into the crystal goblets, she frowned. It wasn't that she didn't like his surprise, but they couldn't afford it. They'd been at the motel for three days now, and there was still no word on Quincy. Even with only one room, they were bordering on bankruptcy. She'd been trying to find a way to break the news to Ian that she was going to have to do some hustling. Remembering his reaction to her game with Romeo, it wasn't a topic she was eager to broach.

"To us," Ian pronounced as he handed her her glass and raised his in a salute.

Ian's toast was fraught with implications she wasn't about to encourage. Just as she parted her lips to scold him, she looked at his face, and her words died on her lips. He looked so happy that she simply couldn't bring herself to spoil his mood.

"To us," she murmured and clinked her glass with his.

Ian smiled, watching Callie sip her wine. He'd deliberately pushed her when he made the toast. For a moment he'd been convinced that she was going to refuse it. The fact that she hadn't, told him that he was beginning to wear her down.

"I hope you're starving," he said as he set his glass aside and opened the pizza box. "The lady's favorite. Double pepperoni and double cheese."

Callie laughed and leaned over to give him a kiss. "You'd better be careful, Ian. You're spoiling me rotten."

"Good," he replied, kissing her back. "I want to spoil you rotten for the rest of our lives." Before she could object, he quickly added, "Hurry up. It's getting cold, and we don't have a microwave."

"A microwave?" she yelped in horror. "You *never* heat pizza in a microwave. It turns the crust to rubber!"

"I can't believe I've hooked up with a pizza purist," Ian wailed jokingly.

Callie bit into the gooey slice. "Sell my cue. I've died and gone to heaven."

"You also have cheese-and-tomato sauce on your chin." Ian leaned over and licked it off.

Callie melted. There *was* something she loved better than a double pepperoni-and-cheese pizza—he was sitting beside her, bigger than life and so delectable she wanted to eat him up.

"Don't look at me like that."

"Why not?" Callie teased.

"I spent good money on this pizza, and I don't want it to go to waste."

"It won't go to waste. The only thing better than hot pizza is cold pizza."

"I despise cold pizza, and I'm starving. Eat, Callie."

"Spoilsport," she accused with a chuckle.

"Yeah, well . . . Besides, if you don't finish your dinner, you can't have your presents."

"Presents?" she repeated as she stared at him with curiosity. "What presents?"

"Finish your pizza and you'll find out."

"Ian, all of this is really nice, but we can't afford it. We're down to our last penny," she said with concern.

"No, we're not." He pulled out his wallet and tossed it to her. "We're flush."

Callie opened his wallet and looked inside. "Where in the world did you get all of this money?"

"I called my dad and he wired it to me."

"You didn't!"

"I did."

"Oh, Ian, how could you do something like that without talking to me first? Do you know what you've done?"

"Yes. I kept us from starving to death."

"We wouldn't have starved," Callie stated irritably. "I would have started hustling."

Ian's smile was grim. "Exactly why I called my dad. I don't want you hustling, Callie."

"That's what I do for a living!"

"Not when you're with me."

Callie didn't miss the belligerence in his voice. She cursed and leaped to her feet. She recognized he was waiting for her to argue the point, and she wasn't going to do it. Instead she took another tack.

"Do you realize that when your father sent you money, he broke the law? Now he's guilty of aiding and abetting, Ian. And if the D.A. finds out about it, he'll eat him alive."

"Who's going to tell the D.A.?"

"The person who wired the money to you. The person who gave you the money. The bank teller who handed your father the large withdrawal of cash," she said with growing agitation. "And those are just the first people who come to mind. How could you do something so foolish?"

"I wasn't being foolish. I was being selfish and, dammit, self-protective," he replied. Glaring at her, he rose to his feet. "I love you, Callie. I wasn't about to watch you hustle your way through pool hall after pool hall for me. A man takes care of the woman he loves."

"You don't love me, Ian! You just think you do."

"No, Callie. I do love you. I want to spend the rest of my life with you. I want to have a dozen kids with you. I want it all, Callie."

Tears welled in her eyes. Crying wasn't going to help; it was only going to make everything more confused. She had to make him see reason. But how could she make him do that when she couldn't see it herself? Heaven help her! She wanted it all, too!

"Ian, I keep telling you that your feelings for me will change. When all this is over, you're going to look at our time together and be horrified by it. You're going to ask yourself what you could ever have seen in me. You're going to see me for what I am."

"I already see you for what you are," Ian rebutted. "And what I see is a frightened young woman who's had everyone in her life turn against her. I see a young woman who has so much love to give, and is afraid to give it. Because every time she's tried to do so, she's had it thrown back in her face. I'm not going to throw your love back at you, Callie. I'm going to grab on to it and cherish it. I'm going to cherish *you*."

"Oh, God, I'm so mixed up," she said morosely.

"There's nothing to be mixed up about, honey," Ian told her as he drew her into his arms. "I'm only trying to love you. Please stop fighting me."

"You make it sound so simple, when it's so complicated," she whispered, resting her head against his chest. "You think you love me now, but you're not in your world—you're in mine. Your feelings will change, Ian. I know it."

"Why are you so stubborn?" he asked with a heavy sigh. "But never mind. I don't want to argue with you. I want to give you your presents."

"No, Ian. Please, don't," she whispered brokenly. "You've already been too nice to me. I don't think I can handle any more niceness tonight."

"Well, you're going to handle it, anyway," he stated determinedly as he led her to the bed and sat her down. Then he knelt beside her, retrieved one of the boxes from under the bed and handed it to her.

Callie's lower lip was trembling as she touched the bright paper that was covered with violets. Carefully, she untied the ribbon and undid the wrapping because she wanted to keep it as a reminder of Ian.

Pulling out a two-pound box of chocolate-covered cherries, she grinned. "Trying to make me fat?"

"No," Ian said as he sat on the floor and smiled up at her. "But I'd love you even if you were fat."

Sighing, Callie shook her head. "You're so bull-headed."

"That is definitely the pot calling the kettle black," he teased as he withdrew the other box and handed it to her.

It was so small it fit in the palm of her hand. Callie caught her lower lip between her teeth, realizing that this present wasn't as innocent as the box of chocolates.

Her fingers trembled as she unwrapped it as carefully as she had the first present, and she let out a small cry of delight when she opened the box and found a thin gold chain, from which hung a small, round gold ball with the number one engraved on it.

"It's a pool ball," she observed.

"It sure is," Ian said. "Look at the inscription on the back."

Callie did as he instructed. More tears welled into her eyes as she read the engraved message: "You'll always be number one to me. Love, Ian."

"Thank you," she whispered hoarsely, cursing herself for not being able to come up with something more eloquent.

"You're welcome." He rose to his knees and settled a hand on either side of her hips. "How about a kiss of thanks?"

"You never give up, do you?"

Ian shook his head. "I only fight for those things I feel are worth fighting for, and you're worth the fight, Callie."

"If I could only. . ."

"If you could only what?" he prompted when her voice trailed off.

Callie shook her head, not about to tell him that she wanted to believe in what he was offering; that she wanted to hand him her heart; that she wanted to trust in his love. She wanted to give him everything he was asking for and more. But the memory of the look on Steven's face when he'd turned away from her in disgust after learning the truth about her hindered her. As did her memory of the prison doors slamming behind her.

"Love me, Ian." She wrapped her arms around his neck and gave him the kiss he had asked for.

"I do, Callie." As ardently as she kissed him, he still felt her withdrawal, and it hurt him so badly he wanted to sit down and cry.

12

QUINCY STOOD at the window and stared at the flashing neon sign outside the Pot O' Gold Billiards Room. If everything went as planned tomorrow night, then he should be walking through its doors in the very near future. It would be the end of an era and the beginning of a new one.

As he continued to stare at the sign, he remembered how he was when he was young. He'd been so brazen, so filled with his own self-importance. Then Callie had come into his life.

Callie. He knew he'd made a lot of mistakes with her. He should have left her with Lucy—as Lucy had so frequently begged him to do. But he'd always felt connected to Callie. It was as if she were his soul mate, and he'd selfishly kept her at his side. If he'd only known what the future held for her, he would have done things differently. He released a heavy sigh.

Suddenly Quincy needed to talk to Lucy. He dialed her number. Tears sprang to his eyes when she answered. "Hi, cupcake," he said.

"Quincy! Are you all right?" Lucy responded with concern.

"I'm fine, and I'm coming home for good."

"Are you saying what I think you're saying?" she asked hesitantly.

"Yes. I've decided to make an honest woman of you."

He could hear the emotion in her voice when she replied, "Well, it's about time. When can I expect you?"

"I have some business to finish up, so it'll be a few days."

"I love you, Quincy."

"I love you, too, but I have to go. Goodbye for now."

Quincy hung up and wiped the tears from his eyes. He prayed that he hadn't lied to her, because he had a feeling that everything in this hustle was about to go wrong.

IAN AWOKE AS Callie began to shift restlessly in her sleep, looking as if she were struggling with a nightmare. He shook her shoulder and said, "Wake up, honey. You're having a nightmare."

Callie sat up. "It's Uncle Quincy. He's in trouble, Ian. I have to find him."

Ian sat up, too, and drew her against his chest. "It was just a dream, Callie."

"No!" Callie gazed at him compellingly. "He's in trouble, Ian, and I have to find him."

"Honey, we've been sitting here for six days waiting for information on him. No one has seen him."

"But he's in trouble!" she exclaimed hysterically. "I have to find him."

"Then we'll find him." Ian lay down and pulled her to his chest, brushing her hair away from her cheeks. "Calm down."

Callie rested her head against his shoulder. "The end is coming, Ian. Whatever is going on is getting ready to culminate, and I'm scared. I'm really scared."

"Shh," Ian soothed as he stroked her back. "It's going to be all right, Callie. Everything is going to be all right."

Ian was wrong. She had a premonition that not only was everything going wrong, but that this was the last time she'd be with Ian. She kissed him with all the desperation she felt inside.

"Oh, Callie," he murmured roughly when she ended the kiss and began to trail her lips down him. "Callie!" he gasped when her mouth touched him intimately.

I love him, Callie admitted. *I'll never love anyone as much as I love him*. Because she did love him, she wanted this last time to be so special he would remember it for as long as he lived.

Even as Callie was giving him physical pleasure, Ian's mind was tormenting him. He loved her. What would it take to prove to her that she was everything he'd ever wanted in a woman?

It was then that he suddenly deduced that Doc Watson and Dr. Watson were so intricately intertwined that "they" were inseparable. The wary, cynical Doc Watson side of her dominated, and he didn't know if the sweet, shy Dr. Watson could ever develop enough faith in love to entrust him with her heart.

Even now, as she made love to him more intimately than any woman ever had, he could feel her slipping away. What could he do to make her understand that she was essential to his life?

"Callie!" he exclaimed harshly as her ministrations brought him to the brink of no return.

"Love me, Ian," she whispered plaintively.

"Always," he said as he surged into her.

"WHERE IN THE WORLD did you get a master key?" Lincoln asked with surprise as Quincy dangled it in front of him.

"I have my resources," Quincy stated cryptically. His depression of the night before had fled with the rising of the sun, replaced by the thrill of the hustle. He grabbed a road map and spread it out on the bed, tapping his finger against a point on the paper. "Now, here's my plan."

Lincoln and Devon bent over the map as Quincy explained, "We'll park the mayor's car at this phone booth. I'll call the big boss and tell him to be at the phone booth by seven tonight. I'll call him there and tell him to get into the car. You two will follow him to make sure that he comes alone and that none of his people are following him. I'll send him to three more phone booths before I tell him to come to this abandoned house where I'll be waiting for him. After he leaves the last phone booth, you guys call the cops, report that the mayor's Mercedes has been stolen and give them this address. With any luck, the police will arrive shortly after he does." He handed Devon a piece of paper with an address written on it.

"Why do you have to be waiting for him?" Lincoln worriedly asked. "Why don't you just leave the ledgers in the house?"

"Because if the cops don't arrive right away, I'm going to need to stall him. Remember, besides, he's bringing Ian's money. When I wrote those checks, I promised myself I'd get his money back. The big boss isn't going to leave it if I'm not there to collect it."

"I don't know, Quincy," Devon muttered, looking as worried as Lincoln. "I think you should stay away from the house and forget the money. If the cops don't get there right away, he's going to have to drive the car back to town, so they'll catch him then. It's too dangerous for you to be there."

"You two worry too much," Quincy scolded, his eyes bright with the excitement of a good hustle. "What's the worst the guy can do to me?"

"Shoot you," Devon replied.

Quincy chuckled. "He wouldn't dare, but even if he does, don't worry. I haven't used up my nine lives yet."

WHEN HE RETURNED with dinner, Ian anxiously regarded Callie. She had been replaying Quincy's tape since dawn, and her face was drawn and pale. When she rubbed her jaw as if she were in acute pain, his heart went out to her.

He sat down beside her on the bed and turned off the tape player. "Take a break and eat something," he encouraged.

Callie shook her head. "I have to figure this out, Ian."

He caught her hand and pressed a kiss against her knuckles. "If you'll eat something, I'll help you figure it out, okay?"

Callie's stomach was in knots, and she was sure she couldn't get a bite down. Ian looked so worried that she nodded. Besides, she'd listened to the tape so many times that she knew it by heart. She could replay it in her mind while she ate.

Ian handed her a sandwich. While she ate, he tore open the paper bag the sandwich had been in. "Do you have a pen?"

"In my purse."

He retrieved her purse and found the pen. Then he turned on the tape player and began to jot down notes on the paper bag.

"What are you doing?" Callie asked.

"Weeding out the blarney," he answered.

Callie gave a wry laugh. "That's the entire tape."

"I don't think so." He rewound a section of the tape and listened intently. Soon the message had come to the end, and he looked over his notes. "Okay, Callie. I'm going to say some words and I want you to say the first thing that pops into your mind."

"You want to play word association?" she asked dubiously.

"Hey, nothing else has worked, right?" When she nodded, he said, "End of the rainbow."

"Pot of gold."

"Little people."

"Pot of gold."

"Destined for greatness."

Callie's eyes flew wide. "That's it! I know where he is!"

"YOU'RE SURE THIS is where Quincy's at?" Ian asked Callie as he pulled their car to a stop in front of the Pot O' Gold Billiards Room. They'd been driving for the past three hours and it was nearly nine o'clock.

"He might not be inside, but he's nearby, Ian. I can feel him. I can't believe it took me so long to figure out his message."

"You said he'd only told you about this place once, and it was right after he took you under his wing. Seventeen years is a long time, Callie."

"The key was him saying that he was destined for greatness. He may be egocentric, but he's not egotistical. All those years ago, he told me that when he won his first game against a professional, he knew he was destined for greatness. In the world of pool, he is great."

"Where do you stand in the world of pool?" Ian questioned.

"Oh, I'll never be as good as Uncle Quincy. If you'd ever seen him play, you'd know that."

"That wasn't an answer to my question."

Callie glanced up at him, and her heart skipped a beat as she realized that he was asking for a commitment— a commitment that she could never give him. "Now's not the time for this, Ian."

"I think now *is* the time." He drew in a deep breath and said, "I love you, Callie. I want to make a life with you. Can you settle down? Or is the lure of the tables too great?"

"It isn't the lure of the tables, Ian. It's— Good heavens, what's that?" Callie gasped as sirens began to blare all around them.

Ian jerked his head toward the back window of the car as a stream of police cars went sailing by. "It must be an accident."

"No!" Callie's hand flew to her jaw. "It's Uncle Quincy! He's in bad trouble, Ian. We have to follow the police."

"Callie, it's against the law to follow the police. We're sure to be picked up if we follow them to an accident scene."

She grabbed his shirt lapels and gave him a shake. "It's Uncle Quincy, Ian. Follow them!"

Ian started to object, but the wild look in her eyes told him that she wasn't going to back down on this. "All right! Remember, if we're caught, it's your fault."

Callie nodded and began to rub at her jaw even harder. The pain was so unbearable she could barely hold back the tears. "Ian, hurry! Uncle Quincy's in serious trouble, and we have to get to him."

"Callie—" he began. Suddenly their car was nearly on top of the police car that was parked horizontally across the road, creating a roadblock. He barely managed to avoid a crash. "Callie, come back here!" he yelled as she jumped out of the car. She kept on going.

He ran after her, tripped on some tangled brush and fell to the ground as Callie disappeared over a small knoll. "Dammit, Callie! Wait for me!"

She never looked back. By the time he managed to scramble to his feet, a steely voice said, "I'm a police officer. Put your hands on top of your head and freeze."

CALLIE DROPPED to her stomach and stared down at the scene in front of her with apprehension. There were a half-dozen police cars parked in front and behind an abandoned two-story house. There was a man backing in the front door, holding a gun to Quincy's head.

Quincy was a hostage. She had to do something to help him. But what?

She scanned the area, noting that all the exits were being covered, so there was no way she could slip inside. She spied a huge white oak growing at the side of the building and shading a broken window on the second story.

It had been years since she'd climbed a tree, and the limbs hanging close to the window looked terribly scrawny. She didn't know if they'd support her weight. The alternative was to sit there and wait. If something happened to Quincy, she'd never forgive herself for not trying to help him.

She gauged the distance between her and the house. It was a good twenty feet, and nearly half of it was lit by the headlights from the police cars. The house was surrounded by high grass and weeds. She might be able to cross to it without being spotted by crawling through the grass.

She crouched down and started to crawl. She covered the first few yards quickly. Approaching the lighted patch of ground, she slowed her pace. She was concentrating so hard on moving slowly that she nearly screamed when the police bullhorn sounded. She lay still for several seconds, forcing herself to calm down before resuming her crawl.

It seemed to take forever before she finally reached the base of the tree, and she snaked around it so that she was between it and the house. Damn! The branch above her was too high for her to reach. There was nothing for her to use to give her a foot up.

She braced her hands against the thick trunk and peered around it. The only limb low enough for her to grab on to was on the edge of the lighted area. She'd need a good swing to haul herself up, which meant that if anyone was looking her way, she'd be caught.

She inched herself around the tree, reached for the branch, and prayed for success. God must have been listening, because a few seconds later she was up in the tree and climbing.

Again her progress seemed to take forever. She had a few unnerving moments as she worked her way back around the trunk on branches that bowed far too low for comfort. She reached the branch closest to the window, but it was a good three feet above it.

After taking a few deep breaths and saying another prayer, she managed to swing her legs in. Her hands slipped on the branch and she felt as if she were about to fall. Then a pair of large, strong hands grabbed her and hauled her through the window.

"Dammit, Callie, what were you trying to do? Break your neck?"

"Devon!" she squeaked in shock, recognizing his voice but not his speech pattern. Good heavens, what had Quincy done to the poor soul?

"Shh!" he hissed angrily. "You'll give us away."

"What are you doing here?" Callie whispered.

"Lincoln and I are trying to come up with a plan to save Quincy," Devon whispered back.

"Lincoln? Who's Lincoln?" She didn't know anyone named Lincoln. For some reason the name rang a bell, though.

"I'll explain everything later. Stay put and be quiet. Quincy would never forgive me if I let you get hurt."

Before Callie could respond, he had moved away. She started after him, easing along the walls as he was doing in order to avoid squeaking floorboards.

They were nearly at the door when another man entered the room, whispering, "They're in the study. There's no way we can rush him."

"What about distracting him?" Callie asked.

Lincoln started at the sound of her voice, and Devon swung around to face her.

"I told you to stay put."

"Yeah. Well, you know me. I never follow orders."

"Dammit, Callie—"

"Hold the lecture until after we've saved Uncle Quincy's hide. Can we distract him?" she asked, turning her attention back to the other man who must be the mysterious Lincoln. Where had she heard his name before?

"Not without getting shot," Lincoln answered grimly. "In order to get to the study we have to go down a long hallway without any cover. I can't see him checking out any noises. It would make him too vulnerable."

"Well, there has to be something we can do. Take me down there and I'll see if I can think of something."

"No, Callie!" Devon exclaimed urgently.

"Come on, Devon," Callie muttered as she gave him a push to get him moving. "You know Uncle Quincy. He's going to come up with a plan of his own and get his head blown off if we don't come to the rescue."

Devon mumbled a succinct curse before saying, "All right, Callie. But you're not taking *any* chances. Got that?"

"Sure. Lead the way."

A short time later, Callie peered around the edge of the wall and down the length of the narrow hallway. Lincoln was right. There was no way they could rush the man, and if he heard noises, he would be a fool to investigate. In effect, he had created the perfect fort for himself.

She glanced around the room they stood in, looking for something to spark her imagination. It was dimly lit by the headlights outside, and there were no furnishings.

Damn! Quincy had really gotten himself into a fix! She couldn't see how she could possibly help him out without getting herself shot.

Just as she was ready to resign herself to that fact, she saw an old set of fireplace tools and inspiration hit!

"I'll be right back," she told Devon before she tip-toed to the set and examined it. She discovered that the round knobs on the ends of the handles unscrewed, and she motioned for Devon.

"What are you doing?" he asked as he crouched down beside her.

She grinned at him. "I think I'll practice some bank shots."

The look he gave her said he was sure she'd just gone over the deep end as Callie handed him three of the five balls she'd managed to remove. She took the other two and the poker and headed back to the entrance to the hallway.

"I get it!" Devon whispered when she knelt on the floor and laid her two knobs on it side by side. He handed her the others, which she lined up with her first two. She tented her fingers and positioned the poker as if it were a cue stick.

She readied herself to shoot the first ball, which she hoped would bank against the wall and then fly through the door. Then she began shooting the balls in rapid succession.

"What the hell?" a man roared as the balls began zooming through the doorway.

"Got you!" Quincy bellowed. Callie, Devon and Lincoln nearly ran over each other as they raced into the room. Quincy was sitting in the middle of his kidnapper's back, his knee holding down the man's gun arm.

He grinned hugely at Callie and announced, "Now, that, Doc, is what I call shooting the lights out!"

Callie's entire body began to tremble as she stared at him—fear, love and anger merging inside her. "Uncle Quincy, I'm going to strangle you!" she yelled at him. Then she burst into tears.

"You were using Ian?" Callie screeched as she stared at her uncle in disbelief. They were in an interrogation room, under guard, and waiting to make their statements. "How could you do that?"

"For Lincoln!" Quincy exclaimed. "They had him framed, Callie."

"I don't believe this," Callie muttered. "In order to prove Lincoln's innocence, you used an innocent man?"

"I know it sounds like dirty pool, Callie, but Ian was never in any real danger. I had enough proof to get him off. I also recovered the money from my forged checks. If you recall, that's how I nearly got myself shot."

Callie couldn't believe Quincy could sit there, looking so pleased with himself. "I'm not talking about the money, Uncle Quincy. I'm talking about the emotional trauma you inflicted on Ian. He had to put his business up as bail. He was hauled into court. His name was in the newspapers. His reputation was tarnished all because you were enjoying the hustle!"

"Callie, calm down."

"Don't you dare tell me to calm down. What you did is unforgivable!"

"I was trying to help Lincoln."

"That's no excuse, and you know it."

"Callie—"

"Don't you even talk to me," she interrupted as tears welled in her eyes. "My whole life I've looked up to you. Right now I'm so *ashamed* of you that I don't think I'll ever be able to forgive you. Ian is the most wonderful man I've ever met. You had no right to do this to him!"

"You love him!" Quincy exclaimed, suddenly understanding. When Callie turned her back on him instead of responding, Quincy said, "Callie, I'm sorry. I was only trying to help a friend."

"Sorry isn't enough this time," she whispered.

Quincy rose to his feet to go to her, but the door opened and a police officer announced, "We're ready to take your statement, Mr. McKiernan."

"We'll talk later, Callie," Quincy told her.

But Callie shook her head, because for the first time in her life, she saw just how shallow the life was that she and Quincy led. He'd been so enthralled with this hustle, that he hadn't taken into consideration who he was hurting, and that included her. "No, Uncle Quincy. We've said enough, and I want you to stay away from me."

"For how long?" he asked with a definite quaver in his voice.

"Forever," Callie replied, refusing to look at him.

RUBBING HER ink-stained fingers against her pants, Callie restlessly strode back and forth in the holding cell. She hated having her fingerprints taken, hated the mug shots and the humiliating strip search.

She still couldn't believe Quincy had done something so crazy. Each time she went over his story, the more bizarre it became. From what she'd been able to put together, Ian's manager, Lincoln Galloway, had been approached by a man who'd threatened that if he didn't let them use the auto-salvage yard as a chop shop, members of his family would be killed. Fearing for his family, Lincoln had given in.

When Quincy had discovered what was going on, he confronted Lincoln. Initially they had planned to go to the police. Then they found out that the crooks had set up the operation to make it appear that Lincoln was the head of the car-theft ring. At that point Lincoln had taken his "extended vacation," and Quincy had managed to get close enough to their contact to lay his hands on some incriminating ledgers. Before he could use them, the police had raided the salvage yard. Quincy went into hiding and set up his ridiculous hustle, which had—as usual—blown up in his face.

Callie sat down on the cot in her cell. At least Ian had been cleared and was free. Quincy and Lincoln had been booked on several charges. The district attorney was talking about immunity from prosecution if they'd step forward as witnesses. Devon had walked, since the only crime he'd committed was helping Quincy set up the hustle. Ironically, out of the whole motley crew, she was the only one destined to do time. She'd made her choices, and she would have to live with them. She just wished... But she refused to finish the thought. Wishes belonged in fairy tales, and she'd given up on fairy tales a lifetime ago.

"Dammit! What do you mean you can't get Callie out?" Ian roared at his attorney. "We can't leave her sitting in jail! She hasn't done anything wrong!"

"She violated her parole, Ian. No judge is going to set bail. She'll have a revocation hearing in a few weeks, at which time a decision will be made on her case. I can build a good defense for her. Until the hearing, though, she has to stay in jail."

Ian muttered a rude, angry curse as he strode to the barred window in the office they were using. He'd promised Callie that he wouldn't let her go back to jail. How could she ever trust him if he didn't get her out right now?

"I want to see her," Ian said.

"I'm sure we can arrange something later today," his attorney responded.

"I want to see her now."

"Ian, it's three o'clock in the morning. The woman is probably asleep."

"I don't care. I want to see her. I have to tell her what's going on. I have to make her understand."

"I'll see what I can do," he said with resignation. "You wait here."

Ian stared out the window again. He'd make Callie understand. She had to understand. He loved her so much, and he'd promised her that she wouldn't go back to jail. Now he was going to have to tell her that he'd lied.

But he'd visit her every day. He'd bring her flowers and candy and tell her how he was going to court her when she got out. They'd go to expensive restaurants. They'd dance until their feet fell off. They'd go to movies and plays and musicals. They'd—

"You can have ten minutes with her," his attorney announced as he walked back into the room.

Ten minutes?

To his horror, they didn't bring Callie to him, but took him to her. His skin crawled as he went through heavy metallic doors that slammed behind him. By the time he reached Callie's holding cell, he was livid.

"Callie?" he murmured as he stepped up to the bars and gripped them.

She was sitting on a cot attached to the wall by chain links, her knees drawn up to her chest. She slowly raised her head, and Ian's heart broke at the look of weary acceptance in her eyes.

"What are you doing here, Sherlock? You should be home in bed."

"You know I couldn't go home without seeing you. How are you?"

She shrugged. "We stayed in worse joints than this when we were on the run. The only complaint I have is that I don't have a roommate. Maybe I'll get one tomorrow, and hopefully she'll play poker. Did you know that I'm a damn good poker player?"

Ian shook his head in confusion. Why was she talking about poker at a time like this? "Why don't you come over here? I'd like to touch you."

Callie shook her head. "Touching isn't going to change anything, Sherlock. This is what I am, and that's what I've been trying to tell you all along."

"Callie, that's not true, and you know it," he responded impatiently. "My attorney says you have to stay here until you have a revocation hearing. He's sure he can get you off. It won't be long, Callie. A few weeks at the most, and I'll come see you every day."

"No, Ian," Callie said. She had to end it now. She couldn't bear the thought of Ian seeing her like this day after day. "I'm not a charity case, and I don't want your attorney's help. I also don't want you coming to see me. It's over between us, so go out and find the woman of your dreams."

"You *are* the woman of my dreams," he stated passionately.

"No. I'm an ex-con and a pool hustler." She threw her arms wide to encompass the holding cell. "Right now, you feel sorry for me. But as time passes, you're going to learn to hate me."

"Callie, that's not true. I could never hate you. And if you'd give me a chance to prove it—"

"No," she interrupted. Her voice was so cold, Ian shivered. "Take your attorney and leave. I don't want to see you again, Ian. Not ever."

Ian saw the guard approaching and fought against the panic rising inside him. He had to reach her, and he had to reach her now.

"Let my attorney help you, Callie," he urged pleadingly. "Then, when you're out of here we'll talk, and I know you'll feel differently."

Callie shook her head forcefully. "No to both, Ian."

Ian's temper flared, but he forced himself to speak calmly, reasonably. "Callie, if you don't let my attorney help you, you're going to go back to prison, and I won't be able to live with myself if that happens. Let him help you."

For a moment, he thought she'd refuse again, but then she said, "All right, Ian. I'll accept his help if you promise you'll never come near me again."

"Callie, I can't promise that."

"Then I can't accept your attorney's help."

Ian wanted to argue further, but the guard arrived and announced, "I'm sorry, Mr. Sherlock, but your time is up."

Ian stared at Callie. She stared back with steely determination. Clearly she wasn't going to relent. Resigned, he dropped his hands from the bars.

"All right, Callie. If that's what it will take for you to help yourself, then I'll stay away from you."

"Thanks, Sherlock. Have a good life."

"You, too." He turned away before she could see his tears.

Callie fixed on the spot where Ian had stood. Her heart was hurting so badly that she was certain she was going to die. She'd done the right thing. Ian belonged to a world that would never accept her. No matter how much he thought he loved her now, she had to end it. She'd had to!

Her vow didn't take away the pain, and she curled into a fetal position on the cot and wept.

TWO MONTHS LATER, Callie was playing the most competitive game of pool she'd ever played in her life. Why had she given up on the sexy clothes? As she made her shot, she admitted that since Ian, she couldn't expose her body as a means of gaining the advantage.

In three more shots, she won the game and her opponent tossed his twenty-dollar bill on the table. Callie reluctantly stuffed it into her purse. The thrill of the hustle was gone, and she'd applied for a position at a botanical garden. If she got it, her pool-hustling days would be over.

Until that happened, she filled her lonely hours haunting Kelly's. She racked the balls and started playing a solo game. She made the break and bent over the table, sighting on the nine ball.

"You'll never sink it from that angle," Ian drawled.

Callie was sure she was dreaming. Slowly she raised her head. Her eyes climbed from his waist to his face, confirming her worst fear. She was more in love with him than ever.

She asked briskly, "What are you doing here, Sherlock?"

"Lucy sent me," he answered. "She's beside herself that you refuse to be her maid of honor."

Callie dropped her gaze back to the table. "Well, considering who she's marrying, I'm sure you can understand my decision."

"Quincy loves you, Callie."

"Is that why he almost landed me back in prison?"

"He was trying to protect you."

"Yeah. With family like that, who needs enemies?"

"Don't you think it's time you forgave him?"

Callie scowled. "Would you?"

"I already have. Quincy is going to be the manager of my newest salvage yard."

"You're a sucker, Sherlock."

"Maybe." When she didn't respond, he said, "I love you, and I want to marry you."

"Don't start," she whispered plaintively. "Please, Ian, just turn around and walk out of here."

He shook his head. "You kept telling me that when I was away from you my feelings would change. It's been two months, Callie, and I love you more with each passing day." When she again didn't answer, he said, "I've told everyone about you. My family and friends are dying to meet you. They think you're a heroine."

"I'm no heroine, Ian," she replied with an unlady-like snort. "I'm an ex-con and a pool hustler."

He reached across the table and caught the gold ball that dangled from her neck. "You're wearing my necklace. Do you ever take it off?"

Callie hadn't taken it off since she'd gotten out of jail. "What do you want from me?"

"Your love."

She gazed up at him through tear-filled eyes. "It can't work, Ian. Even if your friends and family accept me, what if we have children? How do we explain to them that I'm an ex-con?"

"We'll tell them the truth."

"You make it sound so simple!"

"It *is* simple." He rounded the table and laid his hand against her cheek. "I'm dying without you, honey, and I'd bet you're dying without me. Give us a chance."

"I can't," Callie said, tears running down her face. "I'm afraid."

"Oh, sweetheart, I'm afraid, too," Ian whispered as he pulled her into his arms. "I'm afraid that I can't make you see how much I love you. I'm so afraid that you'll keep running without giving us a chance. Please, trust me enough to try. If you can take that one step, I promise you won't regret it."

Callie eased out of his embrace. She latched on to the one excuse guaranteed to send him running out the door. "I can never give up pool, Ian."

Ian smiled and shook his head, as though greatly amused by her statement. "I don't expect you to give it up. I just don't want you hustling. Become a legitimate professional and play all the tournaments you want."

"You'll have crazy Uncle Quincy for an uncle-in-law," she pointed out—that threat should definitely send him running for the door.

"Well, into every man's life a few crazy in-laws must fall," he responded easily.

"You have all the answers, don't you, Sherlock?"

"No. But I do know that we love each other."

"I never once said that I love you," she reminded.

He smiled and shook his head again. "Actions speak louder than words, Callie, and you told me plenty while we were together."

"You're talking about sex."

"No. I'm talking about love." He paused before saying, "I'll make you a deal. If you can look me straight in the eye and say you don't love me, I'll walk out the door and never come back."

Determined to do exactly that, Callie stared into his compelling eyes. The words just wouldn't come. He'd had two months to think things through, and he was standing there saying that he still loved her. Since she still loved him, she'd be a fool not to take a chance on him. Sure, it might blow up in her face, but then again, it might turn out to be everything he said it would be. She was tired of running. When she'd applied for the job at the botanical garden, she'd done so because it was time she started facing life head-on. If she was going to do so on a professional level, shouldn't she carry it over to the personal level, as well?

"Well, Callie?" Ian prompted, wishing he could read what was going through her mind. Her face was as inscrutable as ever. He knew he'd taken a chance by coming here; it would crush him if she rejected him again. But he was so miserable without her that he'd had to take the chance.

Callie drew in a deep breath and took the plunge. "I love you, Ian."

"Oh, Callie," he whispered hoarsely as he pulled her back into his arms and hugged her tightly. She'd finally spoken the words, and he knew that he'd won the battle. "We can make it work, honey. I know we can."

She tilted her head back and regarded him for a long moment before saying, "I know we can, too. I want to take it slowly, though, Ian. We need more time together. Time where we can really get to know each other and prove to ourselves that we can make a lifetime commitment work. I guess what I'm saying is, would you mind a long engagement?"

"No," he replied. "I'll marry you when you're ready—whether it's next week, next month or next year. You're worth the wait."

"Oh, Ian, what did I ever do to deserve someone as wonderful as you?" she asked as a single tear rolled down her cheek.

He caught her tear with the pad of his thumb. "All you have to do is look in the mirror, and you'll have your answer. And I'm not talking about the outside package, Callie. I'm talking about the inner woman. And she's so beautiful that I'm honored to have her love."

His words touched her so deeply that Callie murmured, "I think I'm going to cry."

He smiled at her tenderly. "Don't do that, honey. Kiss me instead. It's a lot more fun."

Callie eagerly complied with his suggestion, and as she wrapped her arms around his neck and touched her lips to his, she knew that you are what you were born to be. Finally she understood that she was born to be held in Ian's arms.

"INDULGE A LITTLE" SWEEPSTAKES

HERE'S HOW THE SWEEPSTAKES WORKS

NO PURCHASE NECESSARY

To enter each drawing, complete the appropriate Official Entry Form or a 3" by 5" index card by hand-printing your name, address and phone number and the trip destination that the entry is being submitted for (i.e., Walt Disney World Vacation Drawing, etc.) and mailing it to: Indulge '91 Subscribers-Only Sweepstakes, P.O. Box 1397, Buffalo, New York 14269-1397.

No responsibility is assumed for lost, late or misdirected mail. Entries must be sent separately with first class postage affixed, and be received by: 9/30/91 for the Walt Disney World Vacation Drawing, 10/31/91 for the Alaskan Cruise Drawing and 11/30/91 for the Hawaiian Vacation Drawing. Sweepstakes is open to residents of the U.S. and Canada, 21 years of age or older as of 11/7/91.

For complete rules, send a self-addressed, stamped (WA residents need not affix return postage) envelope to: Indulge '91 Subscribers-Only Sweepstakes Rules, P.O. Box 4005, Blair, NE 68009.

© 1991 HARLEQUIN ENTERPRISES LTD.

DIR-RL

"INDULGE A LITTLE" SWEEPSTAKES

HERE'S HOW THE SWEEPSTAKES WORKS

NO PURCHASE NECESSARY

To enter each drawing, complete the appropriate Official Entry Form or a 3" by 5" index card by hand-printing your name, address and phone number and the trip destination that the entry is being submitted for (i.e., Walt Disney World Vacation Drawing, etc.) and mailing it to: Indulge '91 Subscribers-Only Sweepstakes, P.O. Box 1397, Buffalo, New York 14269-1397.

No responsibility is assumed for lost, late or misdirected mail. Entries must be sent separately with first class postage affixed, and be received by: 9/30/91 for the Walt Disney World Vacation Drawing, 10/31/91 for the Alaskan Cruise Drawing and 11/30/91 for the Hawaiian Vacation Drawing. Sweepstakes is open to residents of the U.S. and Canada, 21 years of age or older as of 11/7/91.

For complete rules, send a self-addressed, stamped (WA residents need not affix return postage) envelope to: Indulge '91 Subscribers-Only Sweepstakes Rules, P.O. Box 4005, Blair, NE 68009.

© 1991 HARLEQUIN ENTERPRISES LTD.

DIR-RL

INDULGE A LITTLE—WIN A LOT!

Summer of '91 Subscribers-Only Sweepstakes

OFFICIAL ENTRY FORM

This entry must be received by: Sept. 30, 1991
This month's winner will be notified by: Oct. 7, 1991
Trip must be taken between: Nov. 7, 1991—Nov. 7, 1992

YES, I want to win the Walt Disney World® vacation for two. I understand the prize includes round-trip airfare, first-class hotel and pocket money as revealed on the "wallet" scratch-off card.

Name _____

Address _____ Apt. _____

City _____

State/Prov. _____ Zip/Postal Code _____

Daytime phone number _____
                                    (Area Code)

Return entries with invoice in envelope provided. Each book in this shipment has two entry coupons—and the more coupons you enter, the better your chances of winning!
© 1991 HARLEQUIN ENTERPRISES LTD.   CPS-M1

INDULGE A LITTLE—WIN A LOT!

Summer of '91 Subscribers-Only Sweepstakes

OFFICIAL ENTRY FORM

This entry must be received by: Sept. 30, 1991
This month's winner will be notified by: Oct. 7, 1991
Trip must be taken between: Nov. 7, 1991—Nov. 7, 1992

YES, I want to win the Walt Disney World® vacation for two. I understand the prize includes round-trip airfare, first-class hotel and pocket money as revealed on the "wallet" scratch-off card.

Name _____

Address _____ Apt. _____

City _____

State/Prov. _____ Zip/Postal Code _____

Daytime phone number _____
                                    (Area Code)

Return entries with invoice in envelope provided. Each book in this shipment has two entry coupons—and the more coupons you enter, the better your chances of winning!
© 1991 HARLEQUIN ENTERPRISES LTD.   CPS-M1